A NIGHT
LIKE NO OTHER

heartache, suffering, and my battle to recovery.

L.M. TYRRELL

authorHOUSE®

AuthorHouse™ UK
1663 Liberty Drive
Bloomington, IN 47403 USA
www.authorhouse.co.uk
Phone: 0800.197.4150

Published by AuthorHouse   02/19/2015

ISBN: 978-1-5049-3750-4 (sc)
ISBN: 978-1-5049-3758-0 (hc)
ISBN: 978-1-5049-3759-7 (e)

DEDICATION

To all my family and friends...

Dawn, Mark, Emily, Kathy, Daniel and Natalie, You
people are what have held me together through out all
of it I couldn't possibly think of a life without you all in
it. Your strength has helped me rebuild my life...

I love you.

Matthew ... The person that I love.
This certain person has helped me gain so much and all he has done
is show me continuous love. I cannot explain to you the upmost thanks I
want to say but even when you read this know that this book wouldn't
have been released without you standing beside me...

I simply love you.

CHAPTER ONE

I got up from my sitting position. I turned my head as I got up from the table where we sat. "What do you guys want to drink next?" I had just finished my second beer, and it was my turn to get the round in for the guys.

Toby nodded to Austin and Joel, indicating to order for them. "Same again, mate." Toby replied. So, I head to the bar to order the drinks we all wanted. After waiting half- an -hour for the drinks, I was served by a lovely girl. She had a white blouse on, a black blazer with white skulls surrounding the blackness, black skinny jeans that highlighted the stupidity of how skinny she was; bright Florissant red hair, and green eyes with a hint of hazel surrounding the irises. She was a natural beauty with a small amount of make- up that helped compliment her eyes. When I had finished ordering two beers, a Jack Daniels and Cola, and Captain Morgan's Rum with a splash of Lemonade, they were then placed directly in front of me. I paid the red headed barmaid £10.54 and made my way back to the guys.

When I returned back to the table, I placed the drinks in front of the guy who desired each drink. One of the two beers was mine, the other to Austin, the Jack Daniels to Toby and the last to Joel. "Thanks mate! It's much appreciated" Austin said enthusiastically, with a smile on his face. Toby and Joel took their drinks, pulled it their lips and lifted their thump in a manner to indicate 'thank you.' I sat down on the seat that I was previously on.

The inside of the bar was like something out of a biker film. People dressed in black biker leather jackets, chains on trousers, big military styled boots. As soon as I placed both feet into the bar, an overbearing stench of hardcore liquor and Ale entered through my nasal passage. It was a smell that not only an alcoholic could deal with on a day-to-day basis. It was an aroma conjoined with the scent of stale sweat odour, dampness, bad breath and sex. Bald headed men and their 'tag along women' surrounded the snooker table and bar. The place needed to be condemned. I had a total of three beers at the bar.

Toby, Austin, Joel and I had only known each other three weeks. We met through a friend we share, Hayley. I go to college with Hayley, we both studied sports science. She was always better at the theory work, having the brains I didn't have. She wasn't out tonight she said that she came down with a bug, so only meeting Toby, Austin and Joel only once before, they gave me the impression that they could be trusted as friends. They all seem reasonably nice, even if I have only met them just the once before. They told me that they have this gang called the Frappes'. They're nothing like the people I normally socialise with. The friends I tend to spend time with wouldn't be in a gang or go causing trouble. But these three were.

Whitstable, it is a small town, everyone knew everyone. I live in a place called Selling. It's only a few miles away. Hayley knew these guys from college, but I seemed to click with them more than she did. They assured me I would have a good time, so I accepted their request by coming out tonight. I didn't understand at that point that they were only acting so cautious because we were around a girl. I really do need to pay more attention to observation. Whitstable isn't an area where people would normally go out for drinks unless you were local, I presumed. The area wasn't derelict. However, it wasn't where the rich came to socialise. I'm not rich, but I wouldn't normally come to a place like this. The bar, from the outside was covered in graffiti. Words were written on the structure, such as; 'cock suckers bar', 'fags' and other hurtful words that could hurt people who 'bat for the other team'. It was also completely run down. I am surprised that the place is still in business to be perfectly honest.

After leaving the bar at two in the morning, and walking just a few blocks down the road, I began to realise what they were really like. Joel ran across the road, without pausing to see if anyone was around. He started smashing his fist into windows of the passing shops, the glass made a deadening sound as it crashed on the concrete pavement. And the other two were acting out, the same as him. Slamming their fists into windows; throwing bricks at oncoming cars. One car had to swerve away from me as it crashed into an Oxfam shop, just yards away from me. The breaks of the car made a high pitch screeching sound, trying to stop from crashing into something. But it was too late. The Ford Mondeo looked in good shape when I first glanced at it. However, only half the car was visible from where I was stood. There was no sound coming from the people in the car. So I ran over as fast as I could to check on them. The car was completely covered with, shelving, clothing of all different colours, glass and other items, the shop had for sale. Where I was standing I noticed that the front was completely smashed to smithereens. Now I realise the car was not in a good shape. I couldn't hear anything coming from the car. So I called out "is everyone ok?" I heard a silent reply. The thought that the police may believe that I had something to do with the situation, ran through my mind, so I refused to contact any emergency help. I immediately felt guilty. I looked at the alleged 'frappes' with pure disgust, as they were terrorising the neighbourhood we were in. There were no other individuals in sight on this particular cold, dark, frosted, early morning, only us and the silent, injured passengers. I could see my fingers turning blue, my eyes burning, speech slurring and the carbon dioxide leaving my lungs, fading into the air.

The thought that the police might catch me, because I was with them, terrified me. I have never been one to cause or start such trouble. This situation was alien to me. Toby looked over his shoulder to see where I was. He noticed I was on the other side of the street, and not joining in on their destruction. I was starring in his direction. All of their eyes had evil written across them, I hadn't noticed it before. Their entire bodies were as muscular as a heavy weight champion. They all obviously worked out to the degree that their muscles were pulsing through their attire. All three of them dressed in black jeans and t-shirt turned, and I knew they would make me do something I wouldn't want to do. 'I don't cause trouble'. I told myself.

I thought of them making me do something that wasn't right to me, made running the only possible way to get out of this. So, I began to run. I ran past the shattered windows of the shops, making me cringe as my feet smashed the glass into smaller particles and past the vehicle that was smashed into the Oxfam shop, still heard silence. I didn't look behind me, I just carried on running and running as fast as I possibly could and as far as I possibly well could to become unknown of the disturbing scene. At that moment in time I thanked myself for taking up sports science, the running exercises' were paying off right

3

now. After fifteen minutes of running, I could feel the alcohol running through my veins. I had only had three beers'. However, it felt like I had twenty. This isn't normal. I could feel my running, slowing and my eye- sight, faint. My legs were beginning to feel like they wasn't part of my body and my eyes; I could see double of everything. My breathing intake began to increase as my running, became slower.

I heard heavy footing gaining up on me as my speed was slowing. It started raining. I felt the raindrops pouring over my face as I tried to run faster. But it was too late my legs gave way from under me. I fell down onto the soaked concrete pavement. My face smashed to the ground with full impact, before my hands could break my fall. When my face hit the concrete, I felt the bone in my nose break. My eyes started to burn with unshed tears. The sounds of the heavy footing were getting closer to me. And as I thought that they were getting closer a voice broke my internal cursing, towards my legs for buckling under me. "They've kicked in!" one of them said as they stood over me. I couldn't make out whose voices belong to whom. "What has kicked in?" I asked. The blood from my nose ran down to my mouth, I could taste the blood as it threatened to enter into my mouth. My body began to weaken even more. All I could hear were grumbles coming from each of them now. The words were slowly turning from audible words to incoherent words. I didn't understand what was happening. I could feel my entire body losing control. There was nothing I could do, but lay there. Paralysed.

My eyes were wide open, but everything was a blur. My body I could feel, but I couldn't move. What do I do? Everything in my gut screaming; run! But I couldn't run. I had to hope that someone would see me and help me. As if reading my mind they took all chances of that away. They grabbed my arms and legs with their tight grip of their hands; they carried me for around ten minutes before putting me down a dark stingy side way alley behind one of the shops. The cold air rushed past my face whilst I took in my surroundings. With hardly any sight, I had to use my hearing senses to build an internal description of my surroundings, because if I was eventually able to break out of this frozen state then I needed to grab as much detail as possible to get out eventually, if I ever do. They took me to the furthest point of the alley. I made a mental note to myself as we passed things that either touched me or I could hear. The only thing

I felt was their tight grip on my arms and legs. And the only sound I could hear was the intake of breath from them. They finally put me down on the ground. No one would help me now. Everything was still unsettling; my breathing began to increase as they started to rip my clothes off. Shoe by shoe, trousers, jacket, socks, t-shirt, and boxer shorts. My head was bobbing up and down as they were undressing me. I wanted to scream get off of me. But I couldn't, I was paralysed. I reminded myself. The thought that someone may come and help me never shifted from my mind. I had to hope, that's all I could do. There wasn't anything I could do.

I lay on the dirty ground, covered in mud and unknown decay of whatever there was. But I guessed it most definitely wasn't crystal clean. They began to kick the left and right side of my body working their way up from my feet and up to my head. The pain was excruciating. I could feel every ounce of conflicting pain that they pursued. My body was limp. I couldn't fight my own battle. I could feel the pain as it surged through me. And then they stopped but the pain was still there cursing through my body.

I felt a tight grip on both of my legs and lifted them towards my face. My knees were at the sides of my head. I felt my hip disconnecting as they pushed harder to force my legs back. My body began to tremble with horrific shivers as the realisation kicked in. The thought started processing slowly through my brain. They are going to rape me! They glared at me and laughed in my face. That face will forever be imprinted in my picture perfect memory. I was, immediately, scarred.

With all the strength I held within my body, I tried to push them away. But I couldn't move. My entire body was frozen, still. I tried to question to why this is happening to me. Surely I should have known this, right? I couldn't recall or answer any of my many questions. The reminiscence of martial arts self-defence rushed through my mind, I couldn't use them, and I couldn't do anything. I was drugged.

I saw a flicker of an image above my face. It seemed like they were laughing but because my hearing was impaired I couldn't make out if they were laughing or talking. The pain never left me. The pain entwined with the thought of what they were going to do to me, covered everything else I thought. I could feel my entire body turning to ice because it was so cold. I was naked on the floor in a dirty alley- way, in the middle of winter. The wind was screaming as it passed the entrance of the alley- way. It was making my ears burn with the bitter coldness.

My mother, when I was at a younger age, always told me to sing when I was in a public toilet. So that when I was out of sight, she would know I was ok. However, now it was impossible to sing, my vocal chords didn't even contract to communicate even a whisper. My mum couldn't hear me, she couldn't save me, and I was alone.

'Shit, shit, oh my shit!' I internally said to myself. There was a sharp stabbing feeling in my anus. I tried to push away, but I couldn't. I had to lie there and let them do what they first intended to do. Which was rape, and kill me? 'Ouch!' There it was again, that sharp stabbing pain. And then it was happening more than just a couple of times, I couldn't breath. It was like they were shoving a ten-foot barge pole up my anal passage. The pain was excruciating. I tried to tense all my muscles so I could prevent them sliding in me one more time. My muscles were the ones that weren't working. I could do nothing until the drugs were out of my system. The pain surged through me one last time before he pulled out of me. And then I could feel the pain as the muscles were fighting to repair themselves by conflicting together. It made no sense to me; I couldn't move my muscles, although I could feel them.

'Ouch!' there is was again. He was doing it again. Or was it one of the other two? I wasn't sure but this time the pain worsened as he forced his hard penis inside me. The pain was overwhelming. 'I want to die' I internally told myself. Death couldn't come sooner. I would rather be dead than feel this pain. I wished for death more than I could ever imagine. He thrust himself inside one more time before getting off me. I could feel all the pain colliding together again. 'Please take me' I prayed to God. At that moment I knew there was no god, he wouldn't let this happen to a person, he wouldn't create such cruelty and evilness.

In my life I've always thought that I was a strong willed person, I would do anything for anyone who needed it. I would be the person people came to when they needed help. But now I needed help and I wasn't getting any. All I was getting was the pain that everyone else had felt and because I helped them, this was my punishment.

'Oh no.' There it was again, that sharp, stabbing, uncontrollable pain came yet another time. I questioned myself some more. When? What? Why? I could feel the pressure of his muscles tightening, sharp nails were digging into either side of my hips, and a burning sensation ran through my body as fast as the speed of light. I couldn't possibly take anymore. I was quivering in pain, stuck and lacked control. I felt my self - esteem vanishing as he finished off his disgusting job. He ejaculated inside me.

The pressure from their hold on my legs, released. Both my legs fell to the ground, in limp condition. He grasped at both my arms with tremendous pressure, pushed them down onto the ground and glared at me. I could see his ugly, dirty face just inches away from mine. He paused, took a breath, looked into my worrying eyes and murmured something. The words that verbally spoke from his intoxicated breath were; 'You deserve this.'

They let go off my arms and they smashed against the dirt on the floor. I was lying naked for the world to see. Embarrassment of that detail was unimportant right now but I couldn't stop thinking it. I knew that someone, who I didn't know could find my body. The monsters stood over me, glaring and laughing. Their laughter became louder and louder until suddenly one of the monsters told them to shut up. Everything turned to silence again. All three monsters glared at me one more time, I heard whispers and saw their heads nodding with agreement. Evil smirks appeared across their faces. I wanted to run but it was too late...

The pain of kicking and fist punching was unbearable. I felt each blow of pain surge through my entire body, they kicked at my rib cage, and it was being smashed into pieces. The pain all at once surged through me once again. I wanted to scream in pain. But the words couldn't come out. I knew I was bleeding from my anus, I could feel it running down my legs. I was un-naturally cold, too cold to even shiver. The pain and the cold integrated within my body. They continued to kick, kick and kick some more with all the energy they had, it enforced as much pain as possible. And then thankfully it stopped.

This made me feel extremely low. Lower than the depth of hell. More questions entered my mind. The same questions anybody would ask themselves. 'Why? What? How?' I could taste my own tears that were streaming from my eyes and rolling down to my mouth. I don't ever cry, I haven't cried since my dog died three years ago, now I was crying because it is the death of me, I am going to die. At that moment, I thought my life was over, well, at least I had hoped it was anyway. Just then I felt my eyes starting to flicker, it was as if I had no energy to keep my eyes open. My muscles went limb, my mouth became dry and my heart started racing like Lewis Hamilton on a F1 race. Maybe this was god's way of giving me my wish, to die.

I couldn't feel anymore.

And I couldn't see anymore.

My body was slipping from consciousness to deep unconsciousness.

I took my last breath.

CHAPTER TWO

Two years later...

Leaving the hospital after three dreadful long weeks; made me hate them even more. The smell of anti- bacterial spray still lingers in my nose, which doesn't help when I am still trying to rebuild my life. Yes, still two years later. 'Pathetic I know'

I woke up a week later after the assault, in an unfamiliar room. The décor of the room was plain white walls; there was a window to the left of my bed lighting up the room with the intensity of the suns raise. I had apparently been in an induced coma for the entire time. For the first time in one week I opened my eyes and looked around the room, not knowing where I was. My mum was in the chair in the corner of the room, her face looked; aged, tired and pain ridden. Realisation settled in, everyone knew what happened to me. I wanted to hide away from the embarrassing feeling within me. I had but myself into a situation that I couldn't get out of, How incredibly stupid of me. At that moment I wish I knew I would now be living with the incredibly, crushing, defined dreams.

My throat was terribly sore; my entire body was aching in pain. Taking a look down my body, I had wires going into my arms and a 'pincher thing' on my finger, later on the nurse told me it was to monitor my heart rate, and the wires were to give me the correct amount of nutrients my body craved for repair. Uncomfortable, was an understatement. My mum, woke from her sleeping state, and then alerted the doctors of my consciousness. As soon as they entered the room they asked me how I was feeling, I replied with a noun, a word that could not describe a feeling, but a word that described me. That word was fine. How could one describe a feeling they felt when they felt nothing at all, there wasn't a word to describe such a feeling. They did some more tests, with needles. I had to cringe away from them; needles are not my strong point. They then explained the intensity of the wounds. I had a fractured skull; broken rib cage; broken nose, and I had to have my anal passageway re-constructed. The pain running through me, I began to understand. I basically had a small amount of bones, still in working order. Due to being left bare in the cold, and wet in the early morning darkness, I was left with the result of pneumonia. With all the physical injuries in count, none of them compared to the mental ones. I couldn't rid the feeling of emptiness.

The bruising covered my entire body. When I tried to move, my body felt like it was a mechanical machine. The doctors also explained the reason why they had to induce me into a coma, it was because my brain had fluid surrounding it, so if I was awake, it wouldn't have given it chance to repair, and there was no other alternative. My mum had to sign the documents as soon as she came into the hospital, giving them permission to do the operations they had to do. The doctor told me I was lucky that someone found me when they did; otherwise I would have died a week ago. I have always wanted to thank the person that saved me, but their name remained, to this day, anonymous. A police officer came to ask for the details of what happened, but my mum told him to get out, and threw the closest thing to her, which was a banana. I turned away and creased away with laughter. Seriously, why a banana? She knew I didn't want to talk about it, and that I would when I when I was ready, and not under any other circumstances. They had to do STI and HIV checks, I had to wait three weeks for the results, they said. Thankfully they did the tests whilst I was unconscious so I could not recall them doing such thing. So by the time I left the hospital I had the results, they came back all clear. 'Thank god.'

When reading a newspaper during my time in the hospital, I felt that I had skipped into the future. The date read; December 1ˢᵗ 2010. Seeing the date made it real, that I was unconscious for such a large amount of time, it felt as if I had a night's sleep, not a whole week. My mind couldn't adjust to the realisation that I had lived through it. I thought I had died. There was no light, only darkness.

When I left the hospital two weeks later after waking up from my coma, they said I had to remain in bed for a month, so that my body could repair itself without causing any strain. I did my best to follow the doctor's orders. However, being a person who has to be motivated constantly, it didn't work for long. My girlfriend and best friend were around constantly to make sure I was listening to the doctors, when my mum and dad were at work. But the time in between, I was trying to do as much as I could, in such a short amount of time. Not walking around was driving me crazy, and the fact that I wasn't allowed to shower myself. I had to have 24/7 care apparently. Alexis, my girlfriend was there constantly even when my parents were there. It was nice to have the company. Elliot, my best friend came around whenever he could, which was mainly at night due to work commitments. I was never alone.

It was nice to have someone there constantly. But I still needed time on my own, I still hadn't let it process through my mind what actually happened. I didn't want it to, because I knew it would make it reality, I didn't want that, so not talking about it was my way of dealing with it. My mum and dad sent me to councillors throughout the last two years. That was only because I didn't speak to any of my friends or family. I didn't see the point in replaying the night, where my soul was taken from me. That would break me, even further than I already was.

In the last two years, I was able to tell the important bits of what happened, so that the monsters were sent to jail. I eventually had to give my statement, although, I only gave enough details to put the monsters away. I couldn't explain the full play —by — play. I couldn't and I wouldn't, it was too soon. When making the statement, I can't remember the name of the police officer that dealt with it. She had long blond hair; tied up in a bun, her face was make- up free, but her eyes stood out the most; bright green eyes stared back at me. She was beautiful, understanding and that made it easy for me to tell the story of the horrific night. The one thing that plays in my mind, still to this day is what she said to me. I asked her why someone would want to do this to me. And she replied with, and I quote; 'It's because of your looks, you're a really handsome boy.' At that point, and still to this day, I wanted to rip my face off. Because of my looks, that was the reason I was raped and on the blink of death. So you can only guess how I reacted.

I would never tell the whole story to anyone; it's for me to hold on to. I don't want anyone knowing the full extent of what truly happened to me. It wasn't fare to place that on some ones head. It will forever be on my mind though, and that's where it's going to stay. I wanted to feel more like a stronger person so I went to the gym daily, I no longer wanted to be scrawny, two years ago I weighed eight and a half stone, and today I weigh; thirteen stone, of hardcore muscle. My chest measured at forty- two inches, tons of protein shakes, an undeniable obsession with weights and running. Although, I may have had the physical body I wanted, I still couldn't erase it out of my head.

I woke with the sun glistening through my bedroom window. The nightmare was exactly the same, as it is every night. Waking up with cold sweats and trembling muscle spasms has now become my way of waking up. Even with an alarm to wake me up, all it does is cut the dream short. Most people wouldn't be thankful that they had been woken up by an alarm. However, for me it was nothing but a relief. I blinked wildly hoping my eyes would adjust to the brightness of the summer sky. I turned to my bedside table to reach for my mobile phone to see what the time was; clicking on the homing button, the screen came to life. "Shit! It's nine o'clock!" I shouted. I quickly stumbled out of bed, rubbed my fingers over my eyelids to freshen my vision. Looking around my room, I noticed a Mulberry duffle bag on the floor, near my computer chair on the far right of my bedroom. When noticing the Mulberry bag I remembered my girlfriend stayed last night. When I made my eyes adjust, I noticed the light was on in my en-suit.

Alexis stood in the en-suite of my bedroom. Placing makeup on her face as if it was a master- piece, she is staring into the mirror. "Alexis why didn't you wake me, instead of doing your 'god dam' make-up?" I glared. My girlfriend occasionally stops over at my house, in a normal relationship the way it happens is to take it in turns. However, with her parents, and I having such different political views, it always ended up as a disaster, so Alexis band me from going to her house. I never complained, but I do wish I could go around more often for her; she does everything for me.

"Alec, I did, you were tossing and turning under the covers, I thought you might be having a bad dream so I tried waking you. But when I did, you pushed me away and told me that you're not at work today!" she shouted back. "So I left you alone." She stated.

"You did, when?" My expression was callous. "About an hour ago!" She shouts, knowing my frustration with her. Well it's not her fault. I shrugged. I have been known to talk fluently with people whilst still asleep, and with no recollection of it the day after, maybe that's what happened?

"Ok I'm going to ring work to let them know that I'm going to be late." I said pointedly, turning away from her to enter back into my room.

"Ok. You do that you ass-hole!" She has a way with words. I love it!

"When you're angry at me, it seriously does crazy things to my mind, you sexy bitch!" I tried to sound as seductive as I could. Taking a step back towards her, I placed my hand on the back of her neck to touch her soft smooth skin, I put my lips to her neck and whispered in her ear "I love you beautiful, I'm sorry baby." I said turning her around to face me; I could see with her facial expression she wasn't going to let this go.

"Alec, I've had enough! Every time you're late for work, you take it out on me, because I didn't wake you, you need to start waking yourself up!" She paused trying to think of the next words to come out. I ran my fingers through her long light brown her and pulled her towards me. Pressing my lips passionately to hers before she could carry on; I felt her lips move to the rhythm of mine, so soft, so delicate, and pure. This is love; this is love that I will hold on to forever. I told myself "Mr Robinson, just because you have the sexiest lips ever!" she placed her finger on her lips. "That have ever touched these, doesn't mean I'm going to forget this!" She said, sending me a wink as she left my room.

Alexis has work, lucky for her she doesn't have to get there until nine thirty, and it only takes ten minutes to walk there. Alexis works as a bar maid in the local bar, south of town. Alexis may work in a bar, but she will not be doing it forever. She is the smartest person I know, she isn't just academically clever, she has a way with seeing things from a different perspective. With what I went through she held on to me for dear life, helping me though the hardest time of my life, it's like she's my air, when she's not around I can't breathe. I know it sounds stupidly ridiculous, but it's true. She has such a strong-minded personality, she has never once thought of herself. Her life remained on hold while I was 'finding myself', she wants to be a doctor, I tried so hard to make her go and get her dreams but she always said 'No, I want to be here for you', that didn't stop me from arguing my point, I didn't get what I wanted though, that girl is all type of crazy for me. I've tried my hardest to make up for her lost time, but to me I owe her so much more, Telling her I love her everyday and doing the things she always wanted me to do, didn't cut it.

So with her literally working only ten minutes away, for me it is thirty minutes, not so lucky for me. I had to be at Top-man in Canterbury at nine. Bearing in mind it's nine miles away. Plus I'm already ten minutes late. So I'm defiantly in my bosses 'bad books.'

It is Time to pick the phone up and dial the numbers in my phone. I hope to god I don't have to speak to my department manger straight away! Please, please, please I pray. I swear she's the daughter of Satan! All she needed were a pair of horns and a large fork. She already has the personality disorder.

The phone rang twice before I heard the receiver being picked up. "Hel-lo Top-man Canter-bury, char-ice speaking, how can I help you?" She said in a stuttering voice, - ah this must be the new girl, obviously unfamiliar with talking on a work phone. - "Hi its Alec, I am a sales assistant there, can I speak to Rachel please?"

"Oh hi; yeah sure." She replied in a hesitant tone, "oh wait, she's in the office, can you tell me how to direct the call up there please?" She said in a shy manner. "Of course." - So I briefly explain how to do it. The new girl managed to transfer the call to my boss. I explained to my boss that I had over slept and I will be at work as soon as I can, she's not in the best of moods with me at the best of times so telling her that I was going to be late made me think I might as well sign my own death certificate! Oh dear lord, today is going to be exciting!

I left my house at 8:15, to go to the job, my mum made me get. I never wanted the job; I didn't want to leave the house even for my interview. The warm heat from the sun was radiating onto my skin, as stepped outside. The one thing that terrifies me most is leaving my house alone. An isolated feeling rushes over me from dawn, until dusk. I would like to say I finally get a break when I am asleep, but I would be lying. The dreams intensify into my darkest fears. The aching pain in my chest from the fear; only makes me weaker, and more of my soul is broken. Each night they remind me of how my life was taken away from me, maybe not in the physical sense, but the mental one. I was never this person before that happened to me. I was strong thinking, strong minded, and most of all I was mentally stable. Well, as stable as any normal person. But I'm not a normal person, not anymore. I'm a person that doesn't know how to actually think for him, a person who was has to rely on others, it seriously sucks! Although, part of me is still that person, I have become a person that lives behind a charade. I lie to my parents and friends every day, by saying I'm ok, I'm fine, and I'm good; all of them lies. I hate deceit; it eats away at me every day.

After eight hours at work, I'm relieved to be out of that place, glad I'm away from Rachel! She makes my stomach turn and annoys the hell out of me, with her demanding tone and her judge-mental personality. Thank god I have a week off work. When she asked why I was late, I replied with; 'I over slept.' At least I didn't lie, doesn't mean she liked it though.

On my way home, back to good ole Selling, I plugged my headphones into my IPhone. I love how when the music is blasting into my ears, the entire world comes to a halt, and I pay no attention to the surrounding people. As I walk to the train station I admire the historic buildings of Canterbury, Kent. It has a lot of wonderful buildings that go back years, even decades. The air is crisp and the breeze is simply divine, just like a glass of wine.

"Alec is home." Is what I say religiously when I entre the house. I looked into the living room where my mum and dad are sitting, I noticed that they are watching a boring documentary about lions; I really do not see the appeal in them programmes. This detached house has been the place where I have lived my entire life; it has been the home for my parents since they both got married at the age of twenty-two. It was built in the late 1800's; the think black wooden beams still hold the internal structure, showing their blackness. Although, being built such a long length of time ago, my dad had the house recon-structured five years ago. My mum and dad both wanted to modernise the internal part of the house.

With the beauty of the house, and all the pleasant happy childhood memories, this house was perfect. However, the bad memories always seem to drown them out. It is a constant reminder that I only live just a few miles away from where the horrific situation took place, I constantly feel isolated due to that horrible fact, and it only intensifies when I'm alone in the house. Getting away would be the only possible way, but I could never leave my mum and dad, I would miss them terribly.

After day dreaming for a while, I realised I needed to find out if Alexis had come back yet. She hadn't text me back so I assumed she would just be here, like normal. "Has Alexis come back yet?" I asked looking at my mum. Her expression indicated she was angry with me. There isn't anything worse than getting a lingering stare off my mother.

My mother's delicate frame is defiantly a charade of the person she truly is. With her frame so delicate, the automatic judgement of my mother would be, timid and a pushover. How people are so wrong it's unbelievable, the people that know her they know to not get on the wrong side of her, including myself. The phrase: 'her bark is worse than her bite' comes to mind when I think of my mother. Even though she maybe just talk she doesn't need to bite, her bark is far worse. But she loves me, she loves me as a mother should, and that's all I can ask of her. She would be the one to make sure I was ok when I am sick.

"No – she – has - not. She will be back soon and when she does come back ya make sure ya apologise ta that young gal. I heard ya shouting at her this mornin'! Next time don't rely on that girl ta wake ya. Ya wake yourself up, ya hear me?" my mother said in her motherly stern voice. Even at the age of twenty-one it still freaks me out.

"Yes mother I will". I reply in an apologetic tone. It's now 7:30 pm; I ran up to my room and threw my satchel workbag down on my double bed with plain black sheets, which are mostly on the floor. I'll clean my room a little, before Alexis comes round, I hope she's not too mad with me; I can't be bothered with another lecture today. So I proceed to tidying my room, when there's a knock on the door. Shit too late!

"Come in!" I shout, throwing my covers completely on my bed.

"Hi, it's me." In a very shy, tone. She walked in and closed the screeching door behind her.

"That door really needs some WD forty on it." I murmured in a nervous tone; not knowing her exact intentions.

"I'll say." she replied, we laughed nervously. She stood in the doorway, waiting for my approval to come in, looking at her face, god she's so beautiful, and she's all mine, with her light brown hair, blue eyes that remind me of the blue of the ocean. There is only one word to describe this girl – perfection.

"Come in baby." I took a deep breath. It's time for me to be the good guy. "So I think I owe you an apology for this morning." I started walking towards her. When I got to her, I grabbed her waist; pulling her against me, I pressed my lips to hers, we moved rhythmically. Slowly I released her, but I kept my hands on her waist. "I know it wasn't your fault for me being up late. I should not have shouted at you this morning the way I did." I said in a sympathetic way. As I look into her big, beautiful, ocean blue eyes.

"Yeah you better be; I didn't deserve that!" She shouted. "I didn't think I would be allowed to come in after you got an 'ear bashing' from Rachael." She made me drop my hands from her waist, so she could walk over to my bed to sit down. I couldn't help but look at that perfectly rounded arse as she walked to my bed! Down boy!

"I know you didn't baby that's why I'm apologising. I shouldn't have shouted at you like that." I paused, taking her in. "By the way you're looking very sensational this evening Ms Reads." I said in a seductive kind of way, taking her in. Alexis is wearing a slim fit, white cocktail dress, which obviously indicates she's going out. Her sexy 'ass' dress wraps around her luscious curves in the most delicate way. Her hair, so beautifully long and light brown tied up in a secure pony - tail style, bright red lipstick, long black eyelashes and her make – up, perfected. She has stunning, natural beautiful skin that is shy of pure whiteness.

"Well thank you Mr. Robinson, I can't believe I could fit into a UK eight; I was rather surprised I'm normally a ten." She sounds astonished.

"So are you off out tonight?" I Murmured, Knowing that she obviously was.

"Yes, me and the girls are off out into town to boogie the night away on the dance floor, I would ask you to come but I think you would feel a little uncomfortable, being on your own, with five girls, maybe some other time?" she sounds very happy that she's going out without me tonight, maybe I should go out too?

"Yeah its fine babe, I'm going out too, so it doesn't matter." I smiled at her trying not to show my lying expression – of course I wanted to go out with her. I don't really plan on going out at all! I worry when she's out, as a man myself I know how the male brain think, "tits and ass." I don't like her to think I'm being controlling, so I just let her do whatever she wants.

She kissed me quickly "I love you baby but I really do need to go, I'm meeting the girls in like five minutes." Looking into her eyes, I pulled her against me, pressing my lips to hers one last time to hers. She strolled casually out of my bedroom door looking back at me to give me a brief smile, revealing her pure white, straight teeth. That smile does crazy things to me! I sat up straight looking at the clock over my laptop desk, trying to determine if I have enough time to call Elliot, get ready and organise a night out. Yes I can do that!

CHAPTER THREE

Automatically, I decide to ring Elliot, my best friend. I've known him since I was three. He and his family moved back to Selling, they moved away before Elliot and I was born and came back for his dads work. We went to school together and the weird thing about it is our mums are best friends too and they have known each other since they were both three too. They have never lost contact with each other. So hoping he's up for a night out, I dial his number and after four rings he answers - "Hey mate it's me, Alec. Do you want to go out tonight?" I asked.

"Yeah sounds good, I'm already on my way out, I'm meeting someone from Sony recording company." Elliot is becoming a first rate artist, I remembered him saying something about a meeting couple of weeks ago, I completely forgot.

"Oh yeah, do you mind if I come or is it a professional meeting?" I tried sounding as interested as I can - I really don't want to stay in whilst Alexis is out, worrying would just cause me to go mental!

"Yeah man, come out with me, I was going on my own." He paused for a moment "I would rather you come with me for moral support, you know, if you don't mind? It's not a professional meeting its just to discuss the tracks on the album I'm writing, hopefully they liked them." Elliot said in a nervous tone.

"Ok mate, I'll be about twenty minutes, is that ok?" I asked.

"Yeah that's fine; I shall pick you up outside your house if you want?"

"Yeah sounds good to me, see you in twenty." The line went dead as I threw my phone onto the bed, and started thinking what to wear. What am I supposed to wear to something like this, casual? Smart? Or both? Yeah I can mix casual with smart, working in Top-man does have its benefits! I thought to myself.

Ten minutes later I've picked out my clothes. My camel coloured chinos, black slim fit t-shirt, blue slim fit blazer and my white and blue boat shoes. I re-did my hair and sprayed some Pacco Robanne fragrance. "God I look good," I say out loud as I looked in the mirror and noticed the outline of my pectorals defined by the material. I grab something to eat, just something quick, ah! A pot noodle will do, something quick an easy! I say to myself, I shrug. I began to wonder what these people would be like. Hmm... I can imagine men in over priced suits with brief cases, arrogant arses that think they are better than everyone else. Oh why did I ask to go? I really need to think before I make arrangements; on second thoughts staying in would probably be more unpleasant thinking of my girl, out clubbing without me, looking so hot, and god damn sexy!

Twenty minutes later the doorbell signalled that someone was at the door. I run down the stairs and shout, "It's for me." and I open the door - it's Elliot, he's wearing navy chinos, blue t-shirt and a black blazer looking very sophisticated. - "Hey how are you? I asked.

"Yeah I'm good thank you, are you ready?" He replied in an enthusiastic voice, he looked like his eyes were about to pop out of head with excitement, oh god a joyful Elliot. It was never a good sign when he came over with a smile so high it reached his eyes.

"Yeah I am; by any chance have you had jelly tots again? You know what they do to you! Have I got a hyper Elliot on my hands?" I teased and laughed, pinching his cheeks. He looked insulted by my comments, I apologised and we head to his Aston martin DB9, yes his dad is loaded, he has his own global business or something, I haven't got a clue about the business, yet he can afford this for his son, so the business must be going well. I'm slightly jealous. Just a little!

When we are in the car Elliot explains where we are going. Which is a nightclub called the London groove; it baffles me because if they need to discuss the album, how are they going to hear each other talk? I decide to ask Elliot. "Elliot; how are you supposed to discuss your album at the Night Club, when the music will be blaring out the speakers?" I said. It's not my contract deal but still, I care.

He shrugs, "Well they didn't say much, just to meet them they're to discuss the songs, so that's all I know really." He replies.

"Oh ok." I murmur.

"Oh and Alec by the way it's in London, that's where we're going." Elliot clarifies. Great! A trip to London: why couldn't it be closer?

Roughly an hour later we pull up in a car park just a few blocks away from the London Groove nightclub. The outside of it is completely white with a devil red door and windows, covering a three story white building, it looks to have an American look, the place is very bold, and bold is defiantly and understatement. The defined white bricks were thick and large, with red framed windows either side of the door. I could hear the music blaring out of the speakers from the outside, as we walk closer to the building.

There are security guards outside the entrance, wearing black suits, and tie, looking very sophisticated. As we line up, Elliot texts the people that we are outside waiting, within a couple of minutes the security people are calling; "Elliot Peterson" out to come to the front, they wave their hands to say go right in. We are then courteously let through without queuing, 'well this has certainly got to be the quickest line I've ever queued in'. I say to myself.

The nightclub is dark, apart from beaming strobe laser lights, pumping with the music. The club was packed with people, to the point where we had to shove past people to get through. We make our way over to the bar, two gentlemen appear at the side of us, they are wearing casual clothes, but looking very smart at the same time, with their slim jeans and shirt, one of the gentlemen looks very familiar. He doesn't look much older than me; he could be around twenty-three, twenty-four? They talk to Elliot but I can't hear what they are saying because of the music blaring through the speakers. Elliot signals for us to follow them, we do as they wish. Passing through the ground of people, I've lost count of how many times my feet have been stood on. Surely we could have just walked around? Obviously not!

So they courteously lead us to what I'm assuming is the VIP area, it's in a room, which has to be unlocked by one of the security guards, and they are standing outside the door. We entered the room with the tall men in suits letting us in first. They held the door open for us. The room was lit with sidewall lights with a tone up or down switch; it was like being in a movie. They had a bright orange corner sofa and the décor was green with a rainbow of floral patterns on the left wall as we entered, it defiantly has a 70's style to it but very modern. The flooring is panelled with oak laminate flooring boards. The main thing that stood out in the room was the extremely large Yamaha grand piano, it was located towards the rear of the room, lit in only a shadow of light, and it was beautiful to say the least.

We all sat down on the orange sofa, I sat next to Elliot where I would feel more comfortable, than sitting next to one of the 'big shots', and the two gentlemen sat next to each other on the other side. They were facing us. The security guy who let us in, had a bottle of chilled bottle of champagne, and poured us all a glass. "I hope you two like champagne; I thought it would be ideal for this evening." The older guy said pouring us all a glass. "Yeah their fines thank you" Elliot said as he took a sip of his glass of champagne.

The man that looks more my age introduced himself first. "Hello my name is Cole Jameson," he says in an American accent, and a tone indicating that we are supposed to know who he is.

"Hello Cole" Elliot paused, after taking a drink, he continued. "I've heard a lot of your music, it's amazing!" Elliot emphasise the word 'amazing'. Now I'm feeling a little uncomfortable, because I don't even know who he is.

The second man said "Hello Elliot, it's nice to see you again." oh that's Mr Green, he helps find unpublished artists, I remember Elliot telling me about him. "I thought we should meet in a more casual setting this time." He mutters, facing Elliot with a yellow teeth showing.

Elliot turned his head and introduces me. "This is my best-friend Alec Robinson; we have known each other years, and I would like his company this evening if that will be ok with you both?" Elliot said in a shy, intimated tone.

"Yeah that's cool man," Mr Green said looking at Elliot and me, with a smile.

I plucked up some courage to speak a sentence. "So Mr Green how long have you been working in the music industry for?" I asked out of curiosity.

He lifted his head up to glance at the ceiling, indicating he was thinking, and began to reply. "Hmm... roughly ten years now, god that's gone fast." Mr Green said as he turned to Cole. "And please call me Carlton, that's my first name, Mr Green is my farther."

"OK I shall ... Carlton," I said, nodding my head in his direction.

"So Elliot let's get professional now." Carlson said pausing to take a sip of his champagne. "We love the songs, and we don't want to change them. However, would it be possible for you to explain why you created such a stunning album? With such intelligence from such a young man?"

There was a long pause before Elliot started speaking. "Well Carlton" Elliot said. sitting up so his posture was straight, showing his professional side. "I have always believed that a song isn't a song without pure meaning behind it. Therefore, when I write, I make sure I pour everything single meaning I have into writing each lyric". Elliot paused. "The point I am making is that when writing an album I can't say what the album its self is about, but I can define each individual song on the album, and tell you about each song. Hence why I've called the album differences". Elliot said turning to look up at me; I'm guessing this is where he needs moral support.

"Carlson, I don't mean to but in" I waited for his approval before I continued. He gestured a smile, and a nod to indicate for me to continue. "Thank you, I've known Elliot for a long time now, like he said previously. However, when I see or hear him write his songs. I see everything that as ever gave him sadness or happiness. I am a big music fan, and to see such defined songs with in-depth purity. I'm sure he will let other people see him for him. He not let you down sir." I didn't mean to sound like a blubbering idiot, but it needed to be said. Elliot wrote about all kinds of things, meaningful things. The main thing that scared him the most was when his mum cheated on his dad. It completely destroyed him, as much as what happened to me. We were both seventeen when we all found out. Elliot stayed at my house for a month, he didn't wasn't to go home. I was the friend who helped him through it, just like he helped me. I guess we both paid each other back now.

"Thank you Alec, but I already know that." Carlson paused to give me a brief smile, and turned his head to look at Elliot. "That would be a good idea, we should organise studio time, and start adding more instruments to it. What I would like to do is keep a couple of the songs acoustic, so that we can show the listeners the song writing talents you have. Would you like that?" Carlton asked with a simple smile.

"Yeah that would be brilliant! I'm free every weekend," Elliot said with a high pitch tone. Elliot works during the week at our local supermarket, he's been working there for around four years now, and still it's not the place he wants to be working.

"Ok I shall get my diary out and book you in, what about next weekend?" Carlton said whilst taking his phone out of his pocket. He started typing numbers into his phone, and then it lit up. He paused, waiting for Elliot to reply.

"Yes, I can do that." Elliot Said with the biggest smile on his face. He looked like he was about to fall if his seat with excitement.

I couldn't believe the atmosphere; it was amazing. All I wanted to do was give Elliot a massive brother love hug. Seeing the realisation that this music thing was really happening for him is crazy. It was the most proud of him, I have ever been proud of anyone in my life. Elliot looked so happy and excited. I have only ever seen him like that when the twilight movies were on. Seriously that guy would have the same grin as a teenage girl at a pop concert; yes it was embarrassing. Elliot's enthusiastic personality always made him stand out to everyone.

"Alec do you fancy getting an actual drink and leave these two ladies here, to talk for a while? I could also do with a cigarette, do you smoke?" Cole said in his deep American voice. He looked at me as if to say; 'I'm bored, help me' I smiled back.

"Yeah I do and ill grab a mojito, see you guys in a bit." I said. He smiled back.

We both got out of the bright orange seating and the security guy opened the door for us both. We headed in the direction of the bar, which was stupidly busy. As we got to the bar the security guy came up from behind me, and signalled for us to move to one side. He led us over to the end of the bar which he obviously made someone serve us before the stand-peed of people, thank the lord! Waiting in that would be like waiting in a Mc Donald's drive through, and that's being pleasant. The barmaid made her way over by daunting those luscious hips and bright red hair, and the biggest eyes I've ever seen. She asked for Coles order and he signalled for me to go first, "I'll have a pint of mojito please." I was shouting at the top of my lungs.

Then Cole ordered, coming closer to the bar. "Yeah ill have the same please and add them to Mr Greens tab" He shouted. Giving her a veneer filled smile, perfect teeth screamed famous person. She didn't hesitate; she made the drinks for us, and then gave us the two pints of mojito we ordered. We took them from her, and thanked her.

"Are you ready to head out side for a cigarette?" Cole shouted. He looked in my direction and took a second look at the security man who was standing next to me. God that guy is tall! It was like looking at a giant!

"Yeah let's go man," I said. Cole signalled that we wanted to go outside to the security guard, and then we started to move in the opposite direction from the way we entered through. I followed them knowing that it was the back door, we made our way out still being escorted by the security guard. The security guard opened the fire exit doors, and we made our way out the building. A feeling of fear swept over me. My throat began to tighten; my knees were shaking. I was alone, alone with someone whom I don't know. I shake my head to pull myself together; I didn't need someone seeing me like this.

As we came through the doors it became clearer that it was more of a fire exit. The railings were inches away from us, and then five steps down to get to the ground of the side of the club. Cole looked at me, and started speaking. "You don't know who I am do you?" Cole said whilst passing me a cigarette. He put me under-pressure immediately. My body tensed the thought of being in such a small enclosed area with someone who I don't know. He's defiantly in my personal space! I backed away.

"Err... What a makes you think that?" I asked stuttering on my words, trying to hide the obvious answer. I didn't know him. He looked familiar but nothing sprung to mind. I only guessed that he was famous due to Elliot's Enthusiasm towards him. I had never seen or heard his name.

He drank some of his drink before he replied. "Let's just say I could tell when I introduced myself. Normally people already have a clear idea of who I am immediately as soon as they see me, but you-" He let the words trail off into nothing. He really is sounding like a complete arse! My mental description was pretty correct, what an arrogant arses. My judgement was, yet, again, correct!

"What do you mean?" My tone was becoming more and more unclipped as the syllables of each word came out. Maybe I should tone it down a little? No that would be too easy for him. Famous people are just people too I, all that is different between him and me, is the amount in our bank accounts.

"You didn't even know who I was even when I told you my name." He said looking frustrated and hurt. What is it about famous people? I swear to god, if Elliot becomes like this I'm going to castrate him!

"How would you even know that?" My voice was becoming angrier. I'm just going to carry on with this tone it suits the situation.

"I could tell by your non- shocked facial expression, that even though I was even in the same room as you, you didn't seem to have the slightest excited facial expression, as usual people." Cole sincerely seemed shocked that I didn't know who he was; it was almost like he wanted to know why I didn't know him. It was very bizarre to say the least. Come on its not like I sit down all day watching music channels and listening to the radio. I'm a book reader for god sake, I find reading a Charles dickens or Shakespeare book to be more mind stimulating, than some teen pop sensation. Although, I would never admit it.

"Arrogant much?" I paused realising I just said that out loud. Shit! 'Word vomit.' his face dropped at my honesty. Good, deserves him right! "I guess I'm not usual, like you said." The anger in my voice was rising. "But no, I don't know who you are. I'm a little dated with the upcoming talent these days, obviously" I paused. "I've been working to much and had no time for a social life, let alone watching or hearing about 'the new music', sorry" I said with a smirk, I was not trying to hide my sarcastic expression.

His face dropped, his facial expression changed, into guilt ridden. "No I'm the one that should be sorry, I shouldn't of bombarded you with questions, I —I just haven't met anyone that doesn't know who I am", - he paused for a brief second, whilst collecting his thoughts "Oh my god, I've just realised how stuck up I've sounded, I apologise." He said in an apologetic tone. Whilst looking down, he placed his hand on his face.

Ok, time to calm this shit down! "Yeah you did, I'm going to be honest, it did come across that way, and don't take it personal but that isn't any way to meet new people". 'I hope this whole night will be over. No, this entire day! WAIT! What the hell just happened, really? I knew I was going to get 'grilled' today, but I thought it would have been by my girlfriend, not a god- dam random person, who I don't even know.' I internally say to myself.

"You know, you are the first person in a long time that has been truly honest with me, most people would grovel to be friends with me. I'm grateful for your honesty I sincerely believe that honesty is honestly the best way to peruse life, even if it does come out a little harsh" Cole Laughed it was like he hadn't laughed like that in years.

I couldn't believe all this was coming out of either of our mouths, or even coming from our vocal chords. This night cannot get any weirder, well maybe this guy isn't so bad after all, in fact if he takes his head out his arse I'm sure we would become good mates. But I cannot deal with people who think they rule the world. That isn't me. "When was the last time you laughed like that? You seem to be laughing like you haven't laughed in a long time" he was laughing still, seriously it wasn't even that funny, or was it? And I just missed the joke completely?

"Sorry, yeah it most certainly has." Cole said still catching his breath from laughing. He threw his cigarette to the floor and stomped it out.

"Shall we head back in now?" Please say yes - please say yes. I repeated. We both finished our cigarettes. When being with someone whom I don't know, in a place I don't know, makes me feel uncomfortable. Cole's alter ego made me forget where I was for a minute, and it all came flooding back to me. I personally would never normally let some self-centred person get under my skin, but Cole Jameson was, like a family of ants crawling there way all over my skin.

He didn't hesitate to answer. "Yeah let's do that, Ashton can you get the door please?" he glanced over his shoulder to me. He knew by my obvious expression. I looked at him with a facial expression as to say, really? You're going to get your security guard to get the door for you? See, no change!

"Oh no it's not what it looks like, he has to get someone to open it for us, and I wasn't being an arrogant arse like I have been just moments ago" He said in a worried tone, with a slight smirk.

"Ok" I said bluntly.

CHAPTER FOUR

Ashton the security guard got the door for Cole and me. He asked someone over the radio called Mac to let us in. We both entered the club again, it was still pounding with music, and still hundreds of people dancing and screaming, making my ears squeal with tinnitus. We forced our way through; well Ashton just towered over everyone so they moved away as soon as they noticed him trying to get passed. So we didn't get to do much pushing. Girls were going wild as they noticed Cole trying to pass through. Cole was acting as if it were his daily routine; I guess it was. We made our way back to the 'VIP' room. Ashton got the door for us and we went inside. Looking around the 'VIP' area, there was no sign of Carlson nor Elliot, but there was the bar maid who served us at the bar just before we went outside, she explained that they went back stage.

"Whys that?" I asked. I looked at Cole to see if he had an idea. He had a small smile on his lips.

"I'm not sure. You're more than welcome to go back stage and see them." The barmaid said in a seductive tone, which I assume was for Coles benefit, more than mine. I rolled my eyes at her.

So we made our way to the back of the stage, being escorted by Ashton. I could get use to this life being shown the easy way to get places, and secrete rooms that no one can enter without a key. As we entered through the backstage door to see them, Elliot was there. A man was putting something in his ear. I was confused. Elliot saw me and shouted; "Alec come here."

"What's up?" I said making my way toward him.

He looks like he's going to jump out of his skin with excitement. "Carlson has got me a surprise gig, apparently this is why he asked for me to meet him here, he wanted to discuss the album and perform. How amazing is that, man?" he said in an Elliot enthusiastic tone (very high pitched, it's like the whole twilight thing again).

"Oh my gosh that's amazing." I said in the most excitable tone I could, I was practically speechless. I looked over at Cole, and he just smiled at me, he obviously knew what was going to happen tonight. But there was still no sign of Carlson.

"Elliot where's Carlson?" Cole said, looking at Elliot.

"He's just about to introduce me. Oh and Alec did you know that he owns this place?" Cole left to find Carlson, and looking briefly back at me with a smirk on his face.

"No! I didn't!" I said surprised.

A man with long black dreadlocks, and casual attire came over and said to Elliot. "It's time." He said, waiting for Elliot to follow him. Whenever I see people with 'dreads' the thought that they can't wash their hair runs through my mind, I always cringe. Personally, I couldn't do it.

Elliot then said, "Wish me luck" whilst following the 'Dreads man'.

"Good luck mate." I shouted so he could hear me.

"Yeah, good luck mate." Cole shouted as he made his way back over to me, and Elliot ran to the stage. Cole looked in my direction whilst walking towards me. He sent me that smirk again.

So Elliot left Cole and I to go on stage, it was like being behind the scenes of a concert. It was simply amazing seeing my best friend on the stage with over two hundred people watching him. I could hear Carlson introduce Elliot and he said; "This young man is going to be in the charts any day soon and you great people have got the first look of this young talented singer/ songwriter. I can see him doing amazing things with his musical talent, he is simply amazing, and here he is singing; 'you know what's inside'. This is Elliot Peterson." Carlson said with pure passion towards music, and Elliot. The crowd went wild, screaming and shouting at the top of their lungs, it was almost deafening. At this moment in time I am the happiest person in the world, not for what is happening to me, but what is happening for my best friend, he deserves this more than anyone. He has fought for this for song long, and now he's getting it. It's true that if you put your mind to something you want to do, you can accomplish anything.

Elliot began singing his song, it was magical, truly magical, the entire crowd was paralysed with silence, and if you dropped a pin you would here it as it fell to the ground. Elliot's voice is amazing, he had a voice like no other person I had heard, it has a husky sound to it, but he could easily go into falsetto with a click of a finger. The amount of runs he did was spectacular, just like he left every note, every lyric clear to the people who was listening. You could feel all the emotion from his voice, the only way I could explain this was, magical. The best part of the song was the chorus, and the last verse. Even though every lyric in the song had a deep meaning, these parts managed to stick in mind. I let my mind drift into nothingness, and blocked everything else out. I let my mind drift...

Eyes are pointing in the wrong direction
Something's telling me
There needs to be some affection
I grab my bags I'm out the door

There's no reason to ask me
You can tell by the look on my face
You know what's inside
This is what my fate has been telling me
For give my mouth
For letting you go
Please think before I leave
I didn't know what love was
Tell me that you believe...
The song was over.

As Elliot left the stage and said good night to the audience, there was an up — raw from the audience shouting 'MORE'! Repeating the words; again and again. They got louder and louder as they shouted. I was standing at the back of the stage laughing, as Elliot made his way over to me. "What did you think of it?" Elliot said, with a gigantic smile on his face.

"I thought it was, shit mate to be honest with you," I laughed indicating I was joking. "No! Honestly it was amazingly perfect," I said honestly. I was so happy for my best friend, he was doing something that he loved, and he was following his dreams, unlike me. Maybe I could take a page out of his book, and learn something.

"You know what Alec, I'm going to perform again, is that ok whilst you wait for me?" Elliot asked.

I paused for a moment to look at the time on my phone. "Yeah sure mate go right ahead I'll be the one shouting the loudest," I said enthusiastically. So Elliot made his way back onto the stage, right where he belongs, and sang another one of his original songs. It was called piano tears. When I thought the last performance was emotional, I was so wrong! The audience was crying and cheering at the same time.

The time is now 00:12am, and time to leave the London groove nightclub after such an eventful night. After getting through the hundreds of people we finally got out the club, but not without almost every girl kissing or hugging Cole and Elliot, mainly Elliot. They were like a moth to a flame. When getting to the pavement there was a large limo waiting outside. "Would you like to come with us? We are just going back to my place, having a few drinks and then crashin' out." Carlson said turning his head away from the driver, to ask us.

"Erm ... would it be ok if we take a 'rain check' tonight, we have to get back, really." Elliot said trying not to offend Carlson. But to me it seems like Carlson just wanted to get back just as much we did, but he was being polite asking anyway. This night obviously made the others tired as well as myself.

"Yeah that's cool man; I'll see you at the weekend. Ill drop you a text." Carlson said.

We both made our way back to his car, not saying anything. Elliot looked guilty for some reason, a reason I didn't understand. We finally made it to his sexy ass car, and he paused before grabbing the door handle to look up at me. His mouth looked like he was about to say something, but didn't. There was still no communication between us. I suppose I should say something, but he's the one that's being bizarre, so why should I make the first move. We got in the car and said nothing.

Weird.

We got to some traffic lights, fifteen minutes after leaving the club. We had to stop because pedestrians were at the crossing. Elliot looked over in my direction and finally began to speak. "Alec, did you see how Cole was looking at you all night?" He said in a shy tone. What the hell is this about? Nope I defiantly didn't see him staring at me.

"No, why was he?" I said trying to keep the hesitation out of my voice.

"Err... YES! Like completely throughout the entire night. It was weird. That's why I said we couldn't go." he put his head down trying to keep his face from me for some reason. He continued. "He was, just weird." The lights turned green, and off we went again.

I looked down trying to grab some thoughts, related to the out of the blue conversation. Nothing came to mind. "Yeah weird" I murmured.

"Alec you seem a little off. What's up? Did he say or do anything to you? If he did you need to tell me now so I can turn around and beat the shit out him." he said in the most aggressive tone I've ever heard, from Elliot anyway. Ok now this is getting weird. When did Elliot start getting weirdly overprotective? It not like anything happened apart from the conversation about how he's a complete arrogant arse, but apart from that nothing. I know Elliot can get protective, but this was still over protective.

"Elliot honestly nothing happened, well apart from me telling him he's a stuck prick, and that if he carries on the way he is, he's never going to have friends." Yep that covers the basics.

"Really?" Elliot said in a surprised tone.

"Yes, really. What's with the whole protective shit?" We both laughed out loud.

"Nothing man just forget it, he just creeps' me out, the way the looks at you." he turned to look out his side window trying to hide his obvious nervous look on his face.

"Like I said, weird," he whispered.

"I'm sorry I left you alone with him, I feel so dumb! I should of thought, but I didn't." Elliot is the most caring person I knew. It was my choice to go outside with Cole for a cigarette, not his. Even though Elliot was caring, he knew how to stick up for himself, and me. Once, when we were in year nine at school, I was walking down the hall —way by the lockers, and this guy called George little bashed me straight into the lockers, I had a massive bruise for weeks after. But Elliot found out about it, and he went all crazy ass on this guy, I wasn't there, but my other friend Allen said it was wicked, Elliot kicked the shit out of the guy, all for me. Elliot didn't care if people called him names or did things to him, but if anyone did anything to me, or any of his friends, that was it, he would go all kinds of crazy!

"Elliot its fine, I was fine." Fine; being the perfect word. I honestly didn't care, because Elliot was having a good time, but the truth was;

I did feel uncomfortable. I never go anywhere without anyone and I ended up getting into an argument with a guy I don't even know. How is it possible I didn't realise until the end? I should have been more aware of what I was doing, because being that dumb before, I ended up getting my soul ripped out of me, like it was nothing.

"Alec, do you really think I'm going to play the dumb ass card? I don't think so. I know you better than you know yourself. So stop the bullshit, I know how it was for you." I didn't reply; he was right.

We spent the rest of the journey home in silence. I really wanted to ask him about how he felt singing on stage. If the saying; you are one with crowed, like all the other artists say when they perform. But nothing was said, I didn't want to go into details of how I was feeling. It scared me. We said goodbye to each other, when he dropped me off at the bottom of my drive- way. I Went up stairs, and straight to bed.

CHAPTER FIVE

I woke after the most restless night sleep. Ever! I really hope Elliot is ok. He seemed really pissed last night. Olly Murs started my day with Trouble Maker coming from my phone indicating I had a call. I grabbed my phone off my nightstand next to my bed and looked at the caller ID. Its Alexis, suddenly, I remembered she went out last night, with her girl friends. I answered the call. "Hey baby, did you have a good night? I missed you," I said sleepily.

There was a long pause. "Erm … Hey Ba - be, yeah I'm good. How are you?" she said in a stutter. Ok something is defiantly wrong.

"Yeah I'm good princess. Are you coming over soon? I'm still in bed naked." I said trying to be seductive, also trying to pull her out of her mood.

"Yeah I'll be ten minutes." There was no seductive tone coming from her. The line went dead. Ok something is seriously wrong. For one, she never leaves a conversation on the phone without saying I love you at the end, and second; she never goes without saying goodbye.

Yep something is defiantly wrong.

Great! What have I done now? I try to think of anything that I did, slightly going crazy in the process, because nothing was springing to mind. Ok so if this has got something to do with me then, I doubt she wants to make love. I got up and dressed. Throwing on whatever was on top of my draws. It ended up being grey shorts and white jack wills top. At least if I'm dressed she not think I want a quick fuck, I hope that will lessen the blow of the argument. What it's about is something I don't know.

There was a knock at the door, ten minutes later. I run down the stairs, and shout. "It's for me." When I finally reach the door, there stands Alexis with inflamed eyes, showing she's been crying. I take her hands in mine, and bring her in. Looking directly into her eyes, I begin to speak. "Princess what's wrong? What's happened?" she didn't reply.

She pulled my hands, indicating to go up stairs with her. When we reach my room she closed the door behind her. All she did was look at the door; I can't seem to see her expression on her face. She turned around, and all I could do was pay attention too, is the tear-socked cheeks and blood shot eyes.

"Alec – baby," She paused for a second to gather her thoughts. "I need to tell you something, can you please sit down." I didn't question the reason why. I sat down at the bottom of the bed.

"What's up baby? Why are you crying?" I started to feel tears building up in my own eyes. Just knowing that the girl I loved was hurting. It hurt me just as much; I hate it with pure passion!

There was a long pause before she started speaking, again. "Baby I don't know how to tell you this, so I'm just going to come straight out with it." She paused again. "I cheated on you last night." She whispered it was hardly a sound. Everything stood still, as the information she told me processed though my mind. All my insides started to clench into a tight grip. My heart felt like it was about to burst out of chest, at any given moment. The pain was excruciating, all I could think about was being sick. With shivering lips I began to speak. "How could you do that to me?" my head fell in my hands as I crouched down to my knees on to the floor of my bedroom, feeling all the pain rush at me at a hundred miles an hour. Looking up I began to speak again. "How could you do that me?" Repeating the same sentence; because she didn't answer. Looking directly into her eyes to see her pain, again. My eyes gave up holding my tears. They started streaming down my face, and on to my shorts. The pain surged through me with full force. I recoiled onto the floor, crouching into a ball as the tears streamed from my eyes.

"You know I didn't do it intentionally, I could never do that too you, for what we have been through together." she murmured whilst putting her face into her hands.

"Well… You should have thought about that before you went ahead, and did it. You don't deserve to bring up our past, if you remember it wasn't you who had to go through it." I paused a moment straining through the anger boiling inside me. "It. was. Me. Who had to go through it, Alexis! You just helped me through it." I paused again. "Alexis, you stand there, bringing things up, that yes you helped me though, but you're your now hoping that is enough for us to get past this. But you didn't realise at the time you would regret it. And now you do." I looked at her with pure anger, and I took a deep breath. "You fucked someone else Alexis and it wasn't me. It has always been you and me, for the last five years. Neither of us has slept with anyone other than each other." She looked directly into my eyes through anger that was building inside her; I could see the strain in her eyes as she was trying to stop her tears.

"Alec" she began. "There is no excuse for what I did, and to make one up to you is worthless, because I know you know me too well." Oh, now she uses the, you know me the most, Excuse me, darling' it's just not going to work! "So I'm not going to. Here's the truth." she started to walk towards me, but I held up my hand to tell her to stop where she was. I didn't want the space between us to become closer than it already was. "I felt like we were drifting apart, and when 'this lad' started whispering sweet things in my ears, I just couldn't resist. I made a massive mistake, and if I could I would go back, and change it, but I can't. I have to live with the consequences, and hope my honesty will benefit the situation I've placed us both in." My memory of Cole saying honesty is honestly the best possibility came to mind, when she mentioned honesty. But the truth was, even though I'm a forgiving person could I get through this? ... 'Hell No!

This has completely destroyed me.

She looked at me and her eyes must have seen the mess she's made, because the tears started streaming from her face, again. Why would she do this to me? All I've ever done is be faithful, and show her every single day that I love her, and tell her I do. Without even thinking about it, I sincerely do with every inch of my being. But this is too much, after everything we have been through together, and she throws it straight back in my face, knowing exactly what it would do to me. It's not only made my heart crumble, but also taken away my masculinity, well the little I had anyway. That got destroyed two years ago. No one deserves this, no one! Trust has always been a big thing of mine, and once it's broken, I can't forgive. I'm a forgiving person, but only to a certain extent. This time it's not going to work.

"Alexis." I began. "I admire your honesty, but this is too much. We have been through so much together, and I thank you for helping me when I wouldn't let anyone else in apart from the girl I love. But you need to realise that, this hasn't just broken my heart, this has completely destroyed me as a man. But..." I paused. "But, you already knew that, because like you said; I know you too well. Not in a million years would I expect you to do this to me. So maybe I don't know you as well as I thought I did. Alexis I love you with all my heart, and this is completely killing Me." she fell to her knees. I could hear the air gush out of her lungs like she's just been hit in the stomach with a baseball bat. I just stayed on the floor trying not to look at her, within seconds I would have ran to her side and pulled her into my arms and tell her everything was ok. I can't do that; I have to stay strong. I continued trying to be sympathetic "You will always have my heart Alexis; I could never dismiss you from my life completely even if I wanted to. Right now I need time on my own, to think things through. Can you please give me that?" I took a deep breath until my lungs were full of oxygen, and then I looked up at her. My heart pounded against my chest as the scene was able to process. She was broken, but I wasn't sure if I could come back from this. I know she could, she's the strongest willed person I know. I was like that once.

She didn't say a word as she got out up, and walked out my door. Her face was expressionless; she gave me a brief nod to show she understood what I needed. When I heard her feet running down the stairs, I had to hold everything inside me back to stop myself from running after her. This is completely killing me. The girl I've loved for the last five years has broken my heart into microscopic pieces. For god sake, I'm twenty-one years old, why on earth can't I act like a normal man, and just get up and get on with it? No! I cannot. This is what love is like. Heart breaking and continuously heart wrenching. I can't have this anymore in my life. I need space from everything and everyone. Life as I knew it was over. The one person I trusted with my life has snatched all of it away from me; I will never trust anyone ever again. It will just be me and only me. I can do this.... I can't do this!

CHAPTER SIX

I let a month past without even blink. That's how it seemed, anyway. I lead the month with utter determination, that I wouldn't let anyone ask how I was feeling. I just didn't want to hear it. With such determination, I wouldn't let anyone show me their feelings towards Alexis and me breaking up. I didn't want to hear the girl's name; as much as it pains me to say such harsh words about the girl I love or loved. I still need to figure my shit out. She texted me every day up until a few days back. She was just explaining how sorry she was and if I take her back she will make it up to me. She obviously got the message then. I didn't want to hear it. I didn't even want to see her or anyone else for that matter. Elliot and his overbearing brotherly love came over a few times to try and pull me out of my misery, but he knew I was in too deep with this girl. So he made up another way to try and take my mind off her, by taking me out. We watched a few movies and went to a pizza place, but that still didn't work. He knew it wasn't working. He just put on a smile and tried his best to get me out of the situation I was in. It was true though, Elliot was the one person, other than Alexis to make me smile and happy. Just by being him, he made it disappear for a few minutes. I was most certainly great full for that. The first conversation I had with my parents after I told them wasn't so bad. I didn't squint once at their reaction. However, my mum isn't going to let this pass, the next time my mum see's Alexis, she better jump in the dearest dust-bin before my mum pounds seven balls of shit out of her.

I didn't leave my room that day unless I needed to urinate, apart from that I didn't leave my room. My mum popped her head through my door during the evening to find out what went down with Alexis and me. She took one look at me and scooted over, and sat on the end of my double bed. She knew exactly what happened as soon as she saw me; I guess it was a mother's instinct, I suppose. "Not again, baby boy?" My mum said giving me a sympathetic expression, what I really didn't need right now.

"Yes mother, again!" I shouted. "Sorry I didn't mean to shout at you". She looked down into her hands. I hated people being sympathetic with me. I like to keep to myself. I hate people interfering into my own business.

"Alec, baby, I'm sorry to hear about her." I loved my mum; she knew not to mention 'HER' name. She knew that I really didn't want to hear it. Well she should, you've gone through enough times! I internally said to myself "I know what this has done ta ya, I don't need ya ta tell me. I'm ya mother. I know everything even if ya don't tell me. But don't let this girl destroy ya. She doesn't even deserve the time or space to think about." she paused a moment. I could see the sorrow for me in her eyes. As much as I love my mum, I really could do without this right now.

"Mum please Stop!" I said, stopping her from continuing. "I can't listen to you feeling sorry for me. It was me who was so thoughtless to think I should trust her, or anyone for that matter, you would have thought that I would get it through my thick scull by now, hey mum?" I laughed out of pure annoyance towards myself for thinking I should trust anyone after the life changing effect two years ago. But no, I still trusted. Not everyone but a person I thought I could. Obviously I was seriously mistaken. I turned to my mum I could see the anger in her face about to explode.

"DON'T YA DARE THINK ABOUT YA- SELF LIKE THAT!" she shouted, no it was more of a scream. I felt my face tighten at the thought of my mother shouting at me. "Ya gave that girl ya trust and yeah she threw it back in ya face, but take this as an eye opener, ya can only trust people, who love you for you. How many times as she asked ya to change your style, ta look like another guys, or ta get ya hair cut like another guy?" she raised her eye -brows. My mum was right, she did, but I didn't care. All I wanted to be was the guy she wanted me to be. I stopped smoking for her, well apart from social smoking. I stopped hanging out with my friends, because she didn't like them. I did everything. I just thought she was being over-protective. Plus the fact she was my lifeline for two years. She held my life together. She wouldn't leave my side, when I was in hospital, for an entire three weeks. Being in a coma for a week was like waking up in the future.

"What's that the fourth girl naw son?" my dad said walking in my bedroom with three cups of coffee and a cigarette. He walked

A Night Like No Other

over to me and handed me one of the coffees and the cigarette. Even though I stopped three years ago, I felt this was the time to start again. Properly

"Yeah dad it is. Don't bother with the sympathy; I really don't want to hear it". I said sternly, making it a fact. Sympathy to me is worse than a being run over by a truck, at seventy miles an hour. I just can't take the sadness from people, especially if it is towards me. I don't deserve it; I never have and never will. Now, that's a fact!

"Don't ya worry, if ya don't want ma sympathy that's fine, ill just be ya dad, and tell ya to suck it up" I laughed at his remark. It most certainly was a dad thing to say in this kind of situation.

"Give me that" pointing at the cigarette, he handed it me, and gave me a lighter as well. I put it in my mouth and sparked it up. I coughed suddenly feeling the smoke entre my lungs and the taste as it touched my lips. It tastes foul! But I knew my taste buds would open up again to the over bearing taste of the cigarette, so I began smoking it.

"Ya shouldn't have given him that, Jake," my mum said, sending my dad a lingering stare. My dad reached for the cancer stick, and tried to grab it out of my hands. I pulled back.

"It's mine, you gave it me," I said pulling the cigarette away from his grasp. I was glaring at him, for trying to take it from me, as if it was a toy your dad gave you when you were five years old.

"So ya have a week off work?" my dad said, obviously changing the subject. He was the best at doing that. My mum and I clashed, a lot. So he would be the one to pull us out of the argument. My mum and I are the most stubborn people in the world, I swear!

"Yeah dad. But I think I'm just going to chill out and relax for the entire week. Is that cool with you both?" I asked hoping they would say yes. To see anything other than this room would just make me even crazier. I needed time to myself to sort shit out.

My mum's facial expression shifted to a sympathetic one "Yeah, but we will be getting' Elliot over!" my dad said knowing Elliot was the best person in this kind of situation. I didn't even want that. I just wanted to be alone! Alone seemed pretty perfect right about now. My parents left my room without saying another word. They could obviously tell by my expression I just wanted to be alone. So that night I went straight to sleep, I wanted to blank everything out.

The third week into the month Elliot dragged me out. I was still doing my 39 hours at work after my week off, working seemed perfect to take my mind off everything, Alexis related. Didn't mean it worked though. All I could think about was Alexis, with someone else. It killed me every time I thought about it. Why the hell is love so god dam painful? I'm never getting in this mess again!

The fourth week I decided, that this was a better time as any to pull my shit together. It had been an entire month! Of just pure morning the loss of something I never will have again. I need to pull myself together. It was my day off so I stayed in bed until ten in the morning. If I ever slept past eleven, I would wake up with the most incredible headache. So, I would always put my alarm on for ten, plus I love having my nightmares broken.

Opening my eyes after being woken up by; trouble maker. I turned my entire body, pulled the covers over me so I was completely covered. I looked out of the window, to see what the weather was like; it was perfectly sunny. What a better English day to sort my shit out. I pulled my hand out of the covers of my black linen duvet and reached out for my phone, what was, as always on my bedside table. I pulled the charger out of its connection, to my phone, and pressed the homing button on my phone.

I had two messages, both were from separate numbers. One was from a number I didn't know asking if I'm ok and what I'm doing tonight. The last one was from Elliot asking what I'm doing tonight and to get my sorry ass together. Nice mate, love you too!

I text back to the number I didn't know, saying, -

I would be a lot happier if I had a drink in my hands. I'm not doing anything tonight. Sorry to be so forward but I don't seem to have this number in my contact list. Who is it? Laugh out loud.

The next to Elliot —

Hey man. Today is de — day I'm going to pull this rollercoaster to a Holt and I'm going to get my freak on. I'm not doing anything. 'Wanna' come over? X

After replying to my text messages I checked the time It read 10; 12, I through my phone on the bed and went in to shower. It feels so good to get in the shower and wash everything away with a nice warm shower to start a new fresh day! But it never really worked, I still felt dirty. After getting out the shower, I looked in the mirror to see what my complexion was like. It wasn't good, might I add. The extent of the morning for Alexis, and the tiredness has gotten the better of my eyes. My face looked aged. I decided to have a shave and make myself look at least a little human. I chose a set of clothes. I really don't care if none of the two people whom text me couldn't make it out tonight. I am still going out. I need a very large pint. I put on my new burgundy knit Jack Will's jumper, my navy denim jeans and my white Van's. Finally after doing my hair into a quiff and looking a little more human like, I grabbed my phone off my bed. I had two new messages one from the number I didn't know explaining it was Cole and wanted to know if I wanted to go and get that pint with him. Weird! How did he get my number and why would he want to go out for a drink with me? I don't even know him, At all. The other from Elliot, explaining he was sorry but he had work until 10pm, and that he will be over at quarter past, Elliot normally just works during the week, obviously they must have been understaffed for him to work on a Saturday. He would normally stay at mine when he came over but not when Alexis was around, they didn't really get along. That wouldn't be a problem anymore. My parents love Elliot so they never had a problem with him staying over. He even has his own key. Walking to my DJ system I plugged my Iphone into the connecting cable, and hit play on my greatest songs playlist. The first song came to life through my speakers was maroon-five, daylight. I clicked back onto the message icon and waited for the messages to come back up on to the screen.

I text Eliot first –

Hey man, that's fine I'll see you later. I'm going out anyway. I'll just make sure I'll be back for when you get to mine. Smiley face. You have a key x

The second to Cole –

Oh, hello. How did you get hold of my number? I can't remember handing it out to you. And I doubt Elliot would of, especially without my permission!

I couldn't remember handing him my number. Why would he want it anyway? Creep! My phone buzzed to life almost straight after I sent the text. It was Cole again.

He said –

I have my ways of getting any number I want. There's that big -headed person again! Sorry if you didn't want me to have it. I need to speak to you. I'm in Canterbury at the moment I can be at yours within an hour. That's if you want to meet up with an arrogant arse? Laugh out loud.

I laughed at the last part, just because he was obviously pointing out the obvious! Do I really want to go out with a pig headed arse? No I most certainly do not!

I texted him back-

I think I'll pass on that. You getting my number from someone without my permission is a little maddening. So I would like it if you deleted it please. Thanks.

Suck on that bitch tits! Why do famous people think that they can do what they want, when they want? It really pisses me off! Maybe he will get it through his thick skull that he's' not the sort of person I want in my life. I've got enough people in my life whom I'm happy with, I don't need anyone else. People just throw it straight back in my face, what's the point?

My phone buzzed to life yet again. Glancing down at my phone it was Cole again.

Do you not want to know my reason why I wanted your number in the first place? I'm sorry for maddening your precious mind! Just get your stubborn arse ready I'm going to be at your house soon. Winky face.

There is no way in hell I am texting him back! Why the hell did he even ask to see if I'm free, when he was obviously going to show up anyway? How the hell did he get hold of my address, and my god dam mobile number! Yes ill meet up with you, you arrogant arse! I will be hitting your face into next year at this rate! I didn't text him back. What's the point? I'm not going to get it through to him, that I don't want to meet him! I jumped on my bed out of frustration and threw my phone at the wall. Getting back up, I grabbed my phone to check it over. Thank god I put a protective cover over it; otherwise I would be looking at a smashed phone right now. Anger never got the best of me, really. But just recently I have been feeling this incredible urge to hit something, or someone.

CHAPTER SEVEN

Around forty minutes later I heard a knock at the door. I started to run down to get it, but my mum got there before I could. She opened the door just as I was about to speak. "It will be for me, mum." I said running down the stairs towards the door.

The door swung open, and my mum's face was full of shock. "Hello?" my mum said nervously. Not trying to hide the obviously shocked expression, and stutter. It surprised me that she knew of him, my mum's genera of music is normally the 80's. Then it dawned on me, his face was plastered all over the world, how could anyone miss his face? 'Well I did.' I said internally.

"Hi Ms Robinson. My name is Cole, I'm here to see Alec." Cole said with a mischievous smile. He was acting as if he was asking his friend to come out to play. Like you do when your ten years of age. My mum didn't reply, for obvious reasons. 'Pull yourself together mother!' I thought. He saw me coming down the stairs. I wasn't even trying to hide my obvious thoughts towards him. I openly glared in his direction.

As I stepped off the last step I began to speak. "Yes mother, this is Cole freaking Jameson. Now put your face back into place and please go back to whatever you was doing." I said out of frustration, automatically regretting the anger towards the women whom gave birth to me.

"Alec you get ya arse in here naw!" my dad shouted, not hiding his stern tone at all! I peeked my head around the corner of the living room door to see my dad sitting on the sofa. He was now openly glaring at me now; His glare was much better than mine. He's had a lot of practice! Karmas a bitch, Alec! "Ya speak ta ya mother like that again, and I will personally see ta it that ya get a good bruising, ya hear me?" yes I most certainly do! I thought to myself. The one thing I hate the most is when my mum or dad shout at me, they have done so much for me and I hate to think I have upset them.

"Yeah dad, sorry I'm just a little short tempered right now." I turned to look over at Cole, to give him a lingering glare. He had that god dam smirk on his face. You wait mate, I'll make sure I wipe that straight off your face!' it thought internally. I turned back to my dad, to continue. "Sorry dad it not happen again." I turned to my mum, and put my arms around her. "I'm sorry mum, I didn't mean to snap at you, and this day isn't turning out as good as I hoped." I whispered into her hair, so she mainly heard me. I didn't want Cole seeing the nice side of me. He's just going to see the kick-ass -side!

"It's ok, baby boy." Oh great now he's going to think I'm some kind of freaking baby! Well I am in my mothers' eyes, but most defiantly not in his! I let go of my mum and she took one glance at Cole, and said. "You are much better looking in really life Cole; make sure you come around again, even if Alec doesn't want you here." Oh great now she's picking sides, and it's not mine! Perfect! Thanks mother!

Cole smirked at me. And then laughed. He knew it would annoy the hell out of me. "I will Mrs Robinson, and thank you." Being nice to my mother isn't going to get you very far, you freak of a man!

Staring straight into his deep brown eyes, I began to speak. "Right! Come on, you've got some explaining to do." I said sternly, grabbing his attention. I walked straight past him into the surrounding daylight, and closed the door behind me. I don't know where I'm going to go, but walking seems like a good idea. I could hear him running to catch up with me. The suns raise was heating up on my face, the ocean blue sky was cloudless.

"You really want me to explain, or do you really want kick my ass?" He said as he caught up with me. He was walking by my side when I reached the corner of Upper Saint Anne's Road.

I didn't stop. "Both!" I shouted. I couldn't help but shout at him. He drives me crazy! People, No! He in general is really starting to piss me off! I've never felt so much anger for one person, who I don't even know. Maybe it was just a face that I automatically wanted to punch as soon as I saw him? I don't know, but it feels right. Still pacing to an unknown place, I began to speak "I hate people that think they can take or do anything they want!" I paused not knowing exactly where to go with this "But you Cole Jameson are pushing all the wrong buttons! And I don't like it, and I don't like you!" Maybe that came out a little harsh, but I meant every word of it. I think I did anyway.

I openly glared at him on my left. He looked like he was in deep thought. He saw me look at him; he looked wounded. Feeling guilty isn't something I feel is going to work for me, not right now anyway! Stopping to a Holt, I turned to look at what he was doing. He looked broken, hurt, pained? I don't know. I'm not use to seeing these kinds of facial expressions. His face was drooped down looking at the concrete ground, and then he looked up at me with curious deep brown eyes

"Alec." He paused. "Why do you hate me? You don't even know me, I thought you didn't judge people?" oh now he's pulling the feel sorry for me card. Not going to happen!

"First of all, you somehow got my number and my address without my permission." I snarled at him with pure disgust "And secondly, you had the disrespect to come to my home without my permission! I have a hard time trusting people as it is, and if you think we can even be friends, you have another thing coming!" I took a deep breath after realising I wasn't filling my lungs to their full capacity. "I hate. That. You. Think. That I will be just another person who will fall to the ground, and kiss your god dam feet, you arrogant arse!" I shouted. Turning back to the road ahead, I continued walking. I heard his heavy footing getting closer to me. He let out a loud sigh when he stood at the side of me.

"I don't think of you like that Alec." He said simply. Oh really? Of course he does!

"Yeah right!" I screamed, putting my mouth into a thin line, showing my frustration towards him. He grabbed my arm, and made me stop. He spun me around so I was facing him. My fist went into a tight grip.

"I'm being god dam serious! Will you just listen to me!" he shouted. The tension inside of me is beginning to grow; if he doesn't let go of my arm soon I'm going to hit him.

"God! Just get it out then! Why would want my mobile number anyway? It doesn't make sense, you don't even know me." I snatched my arm away from his grasp. People were starting to gather in the street, staring at us in our argument. Shit! They obviously know who it is. Their faces as they walked by went into shock as they took him in. I personally didn't see what they were eyeing. All I saw was a guy standing in front of me with dark brown eyes, muscles budging out of his chest, dark brown hair so well kept, he looked like an Abercrombie and Fitch model. WAIT! What that hell am I thinking! I mentally slapped my face, to pull me back to reality. I turned to stop looking at him. I pulled myself out of my confused state, and continued walking.

"Because!" He shouted, his voice echoed to the surrounding houses, and back to us. Everyone stood in shock. 'Gasping coo's and ahhh's' I paused in my tracks, not looking at him, or turning around. All the people in the street were obviously waiting for him to continue. He is a global superstar in selling, Kent, of all places! I don't blame them for staring; if he had the same effect on me I would do the same. But he didn't of course. I was still stood still looking forward. He came up from behind me, and put his hand on my shoulder. "Alec please, just listens to what I have to say." His eyes were full of determination. They seem like they want to tell me something. He looked all around, seeing everyone staring at us, he looked at me, his eyes full and wide, as if he didn't notice before. Why would he? He's got to be use to the over crowed of people by now. I looked at him; his lips began to open indicating he was about to speak. "We need to get off this street!" He said sternly, gritting his teeth together. I nodded in acceptance. I didn't want to be the talk of the street for the next month, let alone the entire of the world!

"Come on, I know where to go, follow me." I said casually. I started to run from the on- lookers. Cole was right by my side running at the same pace as me. No one was following us.

After running for twenty minutes we stopped in a park, south of selling. Nobody came here, and I doubt anyone would look for Cole in this location. It was a little far from the public eye. As we came to a Holt, Cole bent over, and placed both hands on his knees, taking deep breaths. It was as if they were his last. "I haven't run like since football in high school!" Cole stated. Still looking like he was about to fall to the ground.

"That's what you get for smoking." I laughed out loud. And he joined me in a breathless laugh. He straightened up and started looking over at me.

"Right!" he began "Can I please explain why I'm here, please?" Cole asked.

"Yes, please do. I'm dying to know!" I said sarcastically. Making it very aware that I'm not dropping it.

He ran his fingers through his dark brown hair, and placed a hand on his hip. "First of all, like I said I can get any number, and any address I want. I didn't mean, as in I can click my fingers, and I get it, I mean I typed your name 'Alec Robinson' in the Google search engine, and you came up on the screen with your modelling portfolio and it also had a mobile number and where you lived. I remember Elliot saying that you worked in Topman in Canterbury, so I went in to ask them. I spoke to a girl called Grace, I think her name was, and she said that she knew you outside of work, and she wrote down your address for me." Grace is dead when I next see that girl! Grace and I have known each other since I started at Topman; we were on the same training programme. But still, she knows to ask me first. Just because a famous person asked for my address, doesn't give her authorisation to do so! God grace!

"I'm going to kill her when I see her. So what is it that you needed me so badly for? And you do realise that was really creepy, right?" I asked out of curiosity puckering my eyebrows.

"Well I was in Canterbury, on business, and I knew you lived near Elliot, I just wasn't sure how close, and so I had to ask grace to find out. So here I am." Cole said, with a smirk on his face. "I didn't know you did modelling?" Cole asked. I'm not sure saying it I was armature, would cut it, but I could give it a try.

I did modelling when I was eighteen. However, certain circumstances changed the idea of having my picture taken, for work purposes. I had to pull my contract to a Holt, as much as I loved modelling, it was a career I could not be in, not then, and defiantly not now. "Yeah I did it just for a friend, and he posted them online for me." I said. Cole gave me a quizzing looking expression.

"Well I know that's a lie, It came up with the jack wills model Alec Robinson." He lifted his arms in expression. "And there's your face posted on boards all around London town centre." 'Shit! Caught out'! I took a step back.

"Yeah, it's no big deal. I did a few shoots, but that is all. Nothing exciting." Now that was the truth! "So you came here to pay me compliments about me modelling, or were there something else?" I asked out of curiosity, somehow, I don't believe that could be the only reason. I looked into his dark brown eyes.

"Yeah it's nothing big, I just wanted to ask you if you wanted to hang with me, tonight?" Cole lied. I could tell there was something more about the reason why he wanted to meet up with me. Yeah like I want to do that!

I gazed down at the ground and placed my hands in my pockets and straightening my posture. "I don't believe that's just it. You said you needed to speak to me, what about? Spill." I asked.

"That's it." He paused a moment to gather his thoughts. He looked straight at me like it was the last thing he would ever do. "I just wanted to... I don't know. I guess spend some time with someone, that isn't going to look at me like I'm some kind of super hero. I want to feel normal for a little while." yeah right like he could ever, be normal! "I feel like I'm drowning in the public eye. I need to feel normal. I need to be away from it all for a little while. Please, say you will come out with me tonight? I promise to be on my best behaviour!" I could see the serenity in his eyes. I could see the pain driving through him. It was a hard life, I suppose, but why me? Why can't he find someone else?

I decided to ask the question that was playing on my mind. "Why me, Cole?" I asked curiously. If I am going along with this, I at least need a reason why. He burst out into hardcore laughter. Laughing straight into my face like I was missing something, that should be noticeable.

"Why you?" He asked looking at me with a surprised expression.

"Yes why me? And can you please stop laughing in my face. It's making me feel uncomfortable." I could feel my entire face tighten with anxiety running through me. Having someone laughing in my face, it hurt. I can't have someone laughing in my face. It brings on an entire different meaning. I couldn't stand it anymore. I picked my feet up from the cement I felt was holding me down, and shifted my focus to the exit of the park. I ran away from him.

"Alec!" Cole shouted. I didn't turn; I kept on running. "Because it's you, Alec!" He paused, and I stopped running. What was because of me? When he started speaking again, I didn't turn around. "Because you are you, Alec! You see more than the celeb status. You see a guy that is just normal to you." He paused again. I don't care! No one laughs in my face! Not for any reason! "Just please come out with me?" why? Why, would I want to go out with him? All I see is a guy. Who is stuck up and arrogant and... words fail me.

I spun around to glare in his direction. "Fine! I'll go out, but if you act like an arrogant arse, just once..." I held up my finger to indicate one time, and continued. "And I'm out of there, you hear me!" I shouted, a little too loud. He made his way up to me with a smile that stretched up to his eyes, showing his dimples in his cheeks. He came and stood next to me. I'm guessing he was waiting on my next move. "I hate you!" The words came out before I could think. 'God- dam -word-vomit!' I looked down, knowing I didn't mean what I said. Hate is a very strong word, a word I could only use towards a few people. However, Cole isn't one of them. I shuck my head knowing, I was being a dick. I was raking all the hate I had for the world, onto someone that didn't deserve it, a person I didn't even know. He only wanted a friend. I'm kinda' at a loss of them right now, so maybe one can be on the ready and waiting list, for when I'm ready? Maybe.

"Well! You're going to love me by the end of tonight, not hate me. I promise." Cole stated. With a Mischief smile on his lips. 'Yeah, he wishes'! I internally said.

"Yeah, don't count on that Mr super hero!" I paused. I couldn't stop the words from coming out my mouth. "O.M. G. Everyone its Cole Jameson! Ahh!" I shouted waving my arms like a teenage girl at a pop concert. I laughed out loud, knowing it would piss him off. Doing exactly what he didn't expect.

"Ha-Ha! Very funny! Not!" Cole said sarcastically. Giving me a simple smile.

"Yeah. It. Was. Wasn't. It." I mocked. Pointing out his sarcastic tone. "Come on lets go." We made our way out of the park; there wasn't much to say, so we didn't. It was weird talking, or being with someone I didn't know, the feeling of my barrier, came rolling back up, I was safe.

(HAPTER EIGHT

Taking my phone out of my denim jean pocket. I pressed the homing button to check the time. It read 7:03. I turned my head, and started to gaze out of Coles Range – Rover passenger window, and began to reflect on the day. We had spent the entire day chilling. I took him to the local pub just on the high street near the train-station; the pub was called the Red Lion. Before I took him inside, I pointed out that there won't be a VIP area, and it will be full of lunch- time drunks. He didn't seem to care. So after we spent most of the after noon there, I lost count of how many people asked him for his autograph. We managed to get some food and we drank most of the bar, well maybe just me. Cole said he was on some kind of de-tox, plus he had to drive later. So yeah, it probably wouldn't have been a good idea for him to drink much.

Towards the end, it got a little too uncomfortable. There were cameras coming from all directions, they seemed to be getting closer as they went off. So we had to exit through the back. It was pretty exciting planning an escape. I understood what he means when he said that he had enough of being in the public eye. I couldn't do it. Not to that extent anyway. They were like lions stalking there pray. It wasn't a good picture. We managed to make it back to my house in record time, without them following us. Thank god, I know this town. I know all the side alleys and back roads, like they were written on my hand. Cole turned out to be a cool guy, after spending some time with him. We played video games and watched DVD's. It turned out he didn't manage to watch much television, and it was like a major treat for him.

Cole sighed. Snapping me out of my internal reflection. I turned to face his non- expression face, it seems he has something on his mind "What's up?" I asked curiously.

"Nothing. I was just thinking." Hmmm… Nothing? I don't believe that. Not that I care, but its best to ask the obvious question, right? I'm not use to making small talk; I hate it.

"What were you thinking about?" I turned most my body to face him, so I could look as curious as I could. Cole turned his head and looked at me; it seemed he was doing some serious thinking. His forehead was wrinkled from frowning.

"This is a little strong. But I was just thinking of all the mistakes I've made…" he paused to collect his thoughts. "And I seriously wouldn't change a thing that I've done wrong. It's made me exactly who I am today." He said fact over mater. Well if he wants to be open about his life, that's fine, but I'm not. His face changed from determination to mysterious, looks like he has a wall, just like me.

I'm not about to get sensitive. So I did the thing I do best. Get out of the situation I don't like. "Oh – ok. I'll let you to carry on thinking." I said as I turned to look back out of the window and put my hands between the creases of my legs. 'Please don't say anything else!' I internally said. Having other peoples' problems on my mind wouldn't do me any justice. The way I see it is, if I'm not willing to share my life story I wouldn't want to hear anybody else's, either. I don't want to owe them anything.

"It's ok. I'm glad you pulled me out of it…" He paused a moment. "So are you looking forward to the bar tonight? I thought we could grab something to eat as well? I'm a little hungry." Cole murmured and I could hear his stomach grumble as he said the word 'hungry'. I automatically felt bad. I hadn't fed him. We had the food at the red lion, but that was hours ago! Oh Alec, stop being an arsehole to this guy! 'He's done nothing wrong to you'! My subconscious pointed out.

I took a deep breath. Making apologises just aren't my thing. But this guy needs one from me. He's tried his god dam hardest to not act like a dick whilst he's with me, but I just keep pushing him away. 'Am I ready for a friend right now? To even start to trust someone?' I asked myself. I'm not sure about the answer to that, but I am sure this guy needs an apology from me. I turned to look over at him, and I could feel my face redden, by my neglect to someone who was trying to be my friend. I sighed before I began. "Cole…" I began. "I'm sorry for being a complete dick all day. You didn't deserve that. And I'm sorry I haven't fed you, I feel awful." I hadn't noticed while I was speaking, but I basically whispered all of that. I took a deep breath and turned away from him to look out the window again. That wasn't so hard. Not making apologises are not going to change, and I'm certainly not about to change that fact.

"You don't need to be sorry. I understand why you don't like me; I'm a spoilt brat. The truth is even though I know you don't like me, I just can't leave you. And I wasn't hungry until we left your house I was having too much fun to think of food. It's ok, honestly." Cole murmured. What did he mean when he said he couldn't leave me? Is he gay? I need to tell him I'm not!

"Cole…" I paused. Why couldn't I get the words out? 'I'm not gay' this is seriously freaking me out! "Erm… well ok" Oh way to go Alec! Why are you acting like a stuttering fool? 'Man up for Christ sake!' My subconscious glared. I started to fidget in my seat, unable to get comfy. I need to get out of this car. I need space from Mr Superhero! Superhero? Where did that come from? Oh for god sake! This isn't going to be good! I need to change the subject, and quick! "So how do you react to the press all the time? It would drive me crazy, and how far is this god dam place?" I asked. I couldn't look at him, so I stayed staring out of the window, and into the darkness of the streets we passed.

"Well, sometimes it's really cool." He paused for a couple of seconds. "But what you need to realise is, when it comes to a private life, or any life at all, it gets taken over by the press. So my life is on a constant treadmill, I just don't know when I'm going to fall off. So I have to keep my head straight. I think it's like another fifteen minutes away. I don't know much about this place, but I googled it and it seems pretty neat! So I thought I would take you there. And by the sound of your belly, you're hungry so it's good job it's a restaurant until 10:30." I didn't even hear my belly. I didn't feel hungry either, maybe I should eat anyway, and I haven't eaten all day well apart from the meal at the red lion. I just wanted to smoke and nothing else. 'Don't go their Alec.' I said to myself, trying not to think of Alexis. But the truth was I hadn't thought about her most of the day. That felt real good! Every day seemed to be getting harder, but not this day. This day has been good. Maybe disliking Cole was the only way to distract myself. I don't know, but that scares me. How can I spend time with someone that I don't even know? I feel crazy for even thinking it! Yesterday, I wouldn't even have gone and socialised without Elliot. What's happening to me?

The next fifteen minutes we spent talking randomly about how he's finding England. And then he rest of the time it was silent. I don't know what it is about Cole he just seems to pull me out of the 'gutter' and makes me smile, which makes me angry.

Weird!

As we got to the restaurant/ bar, he put the car into park and turned off the engine before getting out; he shot me that smirk again. When we got inside he asked the barman to put us in the VIP area, the barman gracefully went to find out if we could. I never thought I could be happier; I wanted to be away from everyone. Being surrounded by people right now, I really didn't want. I've never been more thankful, when the barman came back to tell us it was available, but for a cost, luckily it wasn't booked out tonight. Cole didn't want to know the price; he just dismissed it, as if it was nothing. He then showed us the way. We sat down at the table, located in the centre of the room, the room was elegantly furnished and decorated, and it was a lot different from the London groove nightclub's VIP area. This place had taupe coloured furnishings, the walls with exotic animals as pictures hanging; the light was a rather large chandelier, which was hovering above the table. The table was set in the middle of the room surrounded by sofas, and in the corner was a mini bar just for this room. Perfection! 'This room is perfect for chillin'. I internally said to myself. I looked over at Cole who was giving me his famous smirk again. And he opened his mouth to start speaking. "So do you like it? I thought being away from the public would be ideal to just chill out"

He read my mind. "Yeah it's amazing!" I said enthusiastically. It was amazing but I still couldn't get Alexis out of my head! I wish this would stop! Why had I put all my heart into something? God dam you Alexis! The good thing about thinking about Alexis was that when I thought about her, it would block out the fact that I was alone with someone I didn't know. It scared the hell out of me that I was alone with someone who I didn't know. His eyes are full with mystery; I wonder what is in that head of his? Not that I care.

CHAPTER NINE

We spent the last hour ordering our food, I had 8oz sirloin, and the trimmings, Cole had beef caesural, which I told him to have, because he hadn't had it before. How anyone could go through out there entire life without trying beef caesural bewildered me. In my family, it was on your plate as young as I could remember; it was one of our family traditions to have it every Friday. And if my mum ever found out Cole had never had it, she would force-feed him for a month at least. Just o he had his life- times worth. 'Yeah. That bad'. We took the rest of the time eating our food and getting to know more about each other. Even though the thought of being so open scared me shitless, I thought I owed him a little, but he did most of the talking, so I just nodded and listened. His family still live over in southern part of California, he come over for work related reasons, and has been coming back and forth for the last two years. As the time progressed, I also learnt he has just come out of a two year relationship to some girl named Jasmine, but it was strictly on the down low from the press. He has a dog called rocky. Whilst we were talking Coles personality started to show through, the real one. He has insecurities, which I don't even have, he didn't mention them, but he didn't have to. He seems to be holding a lot of things back behind his charade; he was holding his guard up, more than me. When I would mention things like; home and himself as a person he would straight away change the subject. Not that it was essential, but none the less, we carried on talking about the differences' of our lives. With him being famous and me just being an ordinary person.

"Alec, you're no ordinary person. For starters your honesty over rules everything." He said. He picked up his pure orange juice and took a sip. The memory of me screaming in his face telling him how much I dislike him, sprung to mind.

I showed him a brief smile and replied, "Thanks, I guess." I said hesitantly.

After a long pause Cole began again "You know when I go back to the states why don't you come with me for a couple of weeks? Longer if you want?" he looked over with a shy expression, wow! He has a shy side! Hmm…. I don't know about this.

"Well, I don't know. I mean let me think about it. When do you go?" Going over to America. That sounds very intriguing. However, spending more time with Cole in a place I don't even know seems a little off balance, because I don't know him all that well. And to just go over to the states like that, would be ridiculous. I have work to think about, and my parents. Would I be able to cope being alone in a place I don't know? No, I would not.

"I'm not sure yet, but if I have to guess then most likely in three, or four months. It all depends on the album, and recording company. I have a few photo shoots in the next two months as well." Cole said, after taking a sip of his pint, and placing it back on the table. His eyes were eager.

"Well if you're not going until then. Will I have plenty of time to think about it?" I asked hesitantly. I'm not sure if this would be a good thing, or bad. I'm not even sure if I want to fine out. I let the thought of getting away from this place rush over me, it seems intensely intriguing. However, I don't think I could cope with being that far away from my parents. Maybe one day, but not right now.

"Yeah take your time. I understand if you don't want to come" Cole said. I could see his eyes were still eager for me to say yes. But I couldn't. Not yet anyway. I need time to talk to Elliot and my parents, and think if this is really what I want to do.

"Ok, thank you." I said. It's not that I don't want to go, because I do. It's just I don't know how to be alone without my parents. Don't get me wrong, I have dreamed about getting away from this place, bringing up all kinds of ideas in my head, but all of them had either my parents or Elliot in them. The plans were never just I, on my own. Even though I would be with Cole, I would still be alone because I don't know him.

The night progressed really well, apart from right at the end anyway. I managed to get so drunk Cole had to help me out of the place. It was extremely embarrassing. As we got through the Exiting doors we were bombarded with flashes in every direction. It was even worse than the pub earlier. I squinted away from them. Cole still had my arm as I leaned against him. I looked straight ahead, and the thought 'we needed to get out of this' came to mind. Cole had his free arm over his face, preventing the press of getting images of his face, and trying to hold me up at the same time. So I pulled myself out of the intoxication, I was in to try and find some balance. I held onto Cole tighter as I pulled myself together. All of a sudden we were running toward his car, running through the flash from the cameras. Before we got to the car he pulled his keys out of his left pocket, and clicked the open button. When we made it to his car he opened the passenger door for me, and said; "Get in." in a stern voice, I didn't argue, I just got in. Noticing the sadness in his eyes, I couldn't take my eyes off him. When he got in the car he put his head on the steering wheel. "Why? Why?" He repeated. "Why do they do this to me?" I could hear the sadness in his voice like he was about to cry. His lips were quivering as the tears were threatening his eyes.

All I could do was sit they're in shock as the cameras, continued. I was shocked at the realisation of what it does to him. He was crushed. He looked up at me; I could see all the hurt gathered in his eyes. It felt like I'd been punched in the gut. "Are you ok?" I don't know why I did this next part, but I did it anyway. I grabbed his hand and placed it in mine. Shocked at the realisation of what I was doing. It felt like there was an electrical surge run through my hand. I still couldn't let go, he needed someone desperately, and I could see it. He tightened his grasp on my hand. "We really should go, they aren't going to stop..." he paused a minute to gather his thoughts. "And I don't really want to be plastered all over the papers." He said. Letting go of my hand. He put the key in the ignition, turned the key and the engine roared to life.

"Yeah neither do I." I laughed nervously.

As we pulled out of the car park at the restaurant, Cole looked over in my direction with a sympathetic smile. His mouth opened to begin to speak "Are you ok?" he said with a worried tone, He then turned his head back to the road.

"Yeah I'm ok, are you ok?" The worry was clear in my voice as well. I couldn't help but feel the need to feel sorry for him. I don't do sympathy, normally. But this guy needed someone. His family was all the way over in America, and he was alone. I know what feeling alone feels like. If my mother found out I just left him alone like this, she would kill me. Well that's what I told myself to stop from running away from him. Seeing him like this was some scary ass shit to put up with!

"Yeah I am. I just hate that my life has to be revolved around other people, other than myself. I hate feeling so isolated, I sometimes feel like I'm drowning in it all. I can see why celebrities turn to drugs and alcohol. But I could never do that to myself, I couldn't do it to my family." I was stunned by his honesty. There was no need to let me know his feelings. That is one thing I do know, not trust everyone, and to keep yourself safe from people who would tell you're deepest darkest secrets, and out you in danger. But he didn't care, he just told me straight out, how he was feeling.

So I began "Cole thank you for being honest with me, but you don't have tell me all this, you hardly know me." I said sympathetically. I didn't want his problems on my head; I have enough already. I'm not a heartless person, but when I have my own problems I don't need anyone's problems to build up within me.

"That's exact the reason why I would tell you these things Alec. You're honest to the point that I can't believe. I can see all the hurt inside you..." he paused; I think to gather his thoughts, I couldn't grasp it by his facial expression, but his eyes squinted like he had something in them. "For whatever reason that is." He paused before carrying on, again. "Well not that I'm saying that there is anything, it's just I can see that your most likely the best person to talk to about things like this, about my life I mean." I looked over at him to give a smile to say he was right about trusting me. But what scared me the most was that he knew something and wasn't about to explain exactly what he knew, or thought he knew. Either of the two, I'm worried. I started to tense my muscle at the thought.

He noticed. "Alec, please don't close yourself off from me. I'm not going anywhere, I promise, and I promise to take care of you." Why on earth would he want to do that? Strangely, it feels good to hear someone say that too me. However, I'm uncertain of the reason why he would want to do that. It just doesn't make sense, not in the slightest.

With a questionable expression, I began to reply. "Why would you want to protect me? It doesn't make sense. Waiting for him to reply, I looked at him with a confused expression.

He shaked his head to rid a thought, and then began to fill in the blanks. "There's no actual reason as to why, I just feel like I have to. It's crazy, I know. Forget I said anything." He changed the subject. "So

57

what has got you down in the dumps today apart from me?" He said with a questionable smirk.

"My girl friend dumped me, that's why." I said causally as if it didn't mean anything. The truth is I don't want him thinking that I'm some weak-minded person; I know I should not have let a girl get so close to me. Truthfully, it did mean something to me.

"Well obviously she's stupid for letting you go. When did this happen?"

"A month ago now. She wasn't just a six-month relationship; we were together for the last five years. It's crazy that I let her get so close to me."

"Ya – no sometime you have to let people in, so you can love them, and they can love you back. It's the way of life. Its shit that people let us down when we let our guards down."

"Yeah, it is." I said simply. I began to think of Alexis, and the way she made me feel loved. It couldn't have been a lie, could it? I know somehow if I were a better boyfriend I would still have her with me. The girl means world to me, the saddest part about it all is, I would still happily die for her. Pathetic, I know. The thing that made me fall for her in the first place was her laughter; it was a true laugh. Not one that you put on to be friendly, it came over the sound of the band that was playing. As soon as I heard it, I wanted to find the girl behind it, and when I saw her, I knew I had to make her mine. I wish she still was mine, but that could never be. She would always be the one that got away. With thinking of the girl that still held my heart, I began to feel emotional. Tears were threatening to shed from my eyes; I blinked wildly to dismiss them. I looked over at Cole hoping he didn't see.

He did. "Alec, are you ok?" He said worrying.

"Yeah I'm fine. I loved her, and she broke my heart. There's nothing else to say really." The truth was now falling from my mouth. I felt liberated for saying it out loud. Why does love have to be so hard? I guess I will never know.

"Well like I said previously, she's stupid for letting you go. You need to find someone that will be looking for you, not the other way around. The person will be everything you need, and want. But she will also have dysfunctions within her personality; it makes us all human. She will come along, don't worry." Coles honest reply, actually made sense, I wouldn't admit it to him, but it did. I don't think I could ever find someone that was as perfect as Alexis. She had the beauty, and the brains.

"Thanks mate." With all these emotions building up within me, I wanted to scream. Why did I let someone get so deep into my life? It was incredible stupid of me, it will never happen again. My chest started to rumble with sadness; tears were flooding my eyes.

"Mate don't let her get to you, she isn't worth it. There isn't a reason to cry, she a stupid bitch."

"I know. But she was everything to me man." Why am I turning into a blubbering idiot? There is only one explanation, the alcohol. Never again am I drinking alcohol. I'm turning into a god – dam girl, for heaven sake.

Tears were streaming down my face; I couldn't stop them. Cole stopped the car, at the side of a road what consisted of nothing but large oak trees. "Please don't get upset." His voice echoed with worry. "…Just look at me." He put his hand against my face, pulling me from my reverie. "Whatever she did, it doesn't matter, do you know why?" I shuck my head indicating I didn't know. "Because you can do so much better." he grabbed my hand, and squeezed it, tight.

"I'm sorry for being an idiot," I said which was barely a whisper.

"Sorry? You're sorry? What for?" He took his hands away from me.

"Sorry for breaking down like that. It's been a long month. Please understand that I don't normally cry like a baby, ever for that matter. Please forget about it, it's a little embarrassing." I didn't want to go home looking like this; my mum would go crazy with worry. "Do you mind if we go for a drive?

"Yeah of course, where do you want to go?" He said, taking away his hands from my face and my hand.

"Anywhere." I replied. I turned to look out the window to see my refection, my eyes were swollen, my cheeks wet, and the sadness still streaming through. For the reason of me crying, it wasn't only for Alexis, it was for a reason much more than that. She held the strength within me for so long that now, I don't even know how to live without that strength. I thrive for it every day, but I know it will never be there for me again. I was alone, alone and waiting for my life to go in the direction of the unknown

After half an hour of pure silence, looking out of the window and taking quick glances at Cole I decided to start to speak. "Cole?" I whispered. "Yeah?" he answered shortly.

"I am sorry for what happened. You shouldn't have seen me like that. It's just been along month and a lot has happened." I said as I turned my head to look out the window again, to stare into the darkness of the road.

"Look at me, Alec." He paused until I turned my head to look directly into his eyes, he continued. "For reasons I don't understand, I feel protective over you. But the weird thing about that is, I don't mind feeling that way, the whole feeling is complete alien to me." He paused for moment. "I first noticed it at the club the other week, my eyes were locked on you." What was he saying? I don't understand. I don't know what to say. Did he really just say that?

So I began. "Well I don't understand either. Especially if you don't know yourself," I laughed nervously. "I do feel like I have known you for a long time, not hours that equal twenty-four hours." I sighed and put my head back against my headrest. Why was I babbling? I can't seem to think straight. I started to fiddle with my finger- nails to distract myself.

"That last bit was a little random." He laughed. "Yeah it most certainly does. I want you to know that you can trust me with any problems. Sometimes bottling things up isn't the right way to approach things." He sounds like my god dam councillor! As nice as it was to hear someone say I can trust him, I couldn't possibly know that for sure. I could never possibly tell him what happened to me, he doesn't need to know, and nor will I tell him.

"Thank you." I said simply. I didn't know what else to say. What can I say? However, it was nice of him to think so positive of him, when all day I have been a horrible person. It proves that you shouldn't judge a book by its cover. Cole had only proven the serenity of his being, there was no badness, and only the badness I had created.

The conversation didn't continue from that point on. Memories of Alexis were swimming around my mind. The way she uses to whisper in my ear while I was sleeping, telling me that she loved me, or when she would relax me when I had woken up from a nightmare. None of that would ever happen again. I needed to stop thinking about her,

I needed to get on with my life the way I did two years ago. But this time I'm going to do it right! I'm going to be the person my parents bought me up to be! Strong willed, and an open loving hearted person.

First I need to let the wall down surrounding me, is that even possible? I'm not entirely sure but there is only one way to find out. I need to start opening up to, and the first person that came to mind was Elliot.

We pulled up outside my house, after Cole asked me if I felt like going home. As we pulled up I decided it was better time as any to thank Cole for listening to my mental break down. "Thanks for listening to me; maybe someday we will get to the point where I can trust you. But that will take time, I don't just give out my trust to people I don't really know." I said. If Cole trusts me with his problems, why can't I eventually learn to tell him about mine? Obviously not the events of what happened to me, but little things that play on my mind.

"Take all the time you need. I will be here. I will earn your trust. I will do whatever you want me to do." He looked at me, and sent me a smirk. This time I had goose bumps all over my arms. What was with this guy? Did I find him attractive? I'm straight though, aren't I? My face was full with confusion. 'Man this is so wrong!' It was silent for a little while, and then he continued. "Hey what's with that look on your face?" he said with a worried tone. What look on my face? And then I realised I was still full with confusion, I laughed nervously. I didn't want him to think I liked him that way. Hell! I don't even know if I like him that way. OHMYGOD! What am I saying? There's only one explanation; I'm going insane.

I felt his hand on mine; I turned to look at him. I realised I didn't answer back from his previous question. "Erm... nothing." I stated nervously. "Thanks for the ride home." When I started to grab the handle, he grabbed me by the arm. I turned around to look at him, I knew if I looked into his eyes that would be it. I would kiss him. 'No I would not'! I told myself. I don't ever lose control, why was I now?

"You can ring me anytime, day or night. I don't care. I'll be here for the next three days. I would like you to take advantage of that, oh and remember to think about coming with me to America." He said. Was he being seductive? Or was he just being nice? Not that I care.

I didn't think; the words just blew out of my mouth like 'word- vomit.' "Yeah I most certainly will." He gave me that smirk again; the dimples in his cheeks were on show. OH. MY. GOD! I couldn't say anything, or look back at him. I needed to get inside, and get in bed, away from him! There is no way I could go with him to America. I opened the door and headed towards my house. I didn't look back.

Two years ago dramatically changed my life. People, for example my parents and the two people that know about what happened, who are Elliot and Alexis. They had always said to me since it happened that I would be able to get over it, in time. That was easier said than done. Two years on and nothing has changed. I still get the nightmares, the images playing in my mind constantly, and trapping away my insecurities'. I don't tell anyone, maybe which is wrong. I don't care though. I don't feel that it's necessary to unload my issues onto someone else. They would think I was crazy. Especially some of the things I think about. Which would include, being scared of walking down the street alone, that I will never be man enough for a women, and knowing I have a play by play of what actually happened. I know it sounds pathetic, but it is the truth. No one needs to know my story. That it is between me, me and me. I know, that feeling attracted to Cole is ridiculous. And out of the question. Not to mention completely and utterly wrong, in so many ways. The feeling that I shouldn't be feeling like this hasn't become un-noticed. Being attracted to a guy, what is that about? I have never found myself attracted to someone who is of the same sex as me. It scares the hell out of me. I need to forget about Cole Jameson, I need to regain my pride and find someone that more suitable for me, Alexis obviously has, why can't I? This is the reason why I need to get rid of him out of my life, completely. Yes, I may have told him that it was ok to contact me. However, now isn't the right time to get emotionally attached to someone that isn't right for me. Even though, I know it will only be strictly friendship based. The other fact that spending time with him would only cause me so many more problems, problems I don't need in my life. I have enough to deal with.

CHAPTER TEN

"Hey, you're finally back." Elliot said as I walked into my bedroom. With all the things I have running through my mind, I completely forgot about him. I grabbed my phone out my pocket. Pressing the home button on my phone it sprung to life, I had three new messages, all from Elliot. Asking me where I was, and that he would be here for 10pm. I looked at the time it read 10:30.

I still hadn't talked to him. "Hey man." I said as I walked over to my chest of draws by my bed, I laid my phone and wallet on them before getting undressed. "I'm sorry I took so long I was out with Cole Jameson…" I paused as I realised he didn't like him that much. I took one look at his face whilst he was lying on my bed with his spider man pyjamas on. Yes spider man, Elliot maybe the best person I know, but he is also the most freakish too. He was right about one thing; Cole was staring at me at the club. He admitted it himself.

His expression changed immediately when I mentioned Cole's name. "Why?" He paused. "Why would you go out with him, Alec?" he sounded surprised. He knew me too well; he knows I don't go out with other people other than him or my parents, to socialise, anyway.

"He asked if I wanted to go out for a drink." I said, trying not to look at him. I didn't want him to see my expression. He would know something was wrong with me immediately. He didn't need me to look at him to know that something was wrong.

"What's happened Alec? You don't seem yourself. Tell me." His voice sounded like it broke in between the lines of each word getting them out of his mouth.

'What's the point in lying to Elliot?' I asked myself. I turned my entire body, looked into his green eyes and answered his question. I told him that I burst out crying in front of Cole. He was shocked that I could even trust someone so quickly other than him and Alexis. But I guess the truth was Alexis had broken my heart, after trusting her with all of my being. She then did this to me. How am I supposed to guess whom I can, or cannot trust anymore? "Elliot…" I paused trying to find words to say to him. "I know this sounds ridiculous, and I know it will to you because you know me better than anyone, but I think I can trust him. Even knowing him for such a short time I feel like I can confide in him." He looked up at me questionably. "I didn't tell him what happened before you ask. That I will need a certain kind of trust to be earned before I tell him; if I ever do. When I told him about Alexis he completely understood and was there for me." I had to push the last remaining letters out of my chest as the tears started again. Seriously what was with the tears and me today?

Elliot looked at me with a shocked expression on his face. His mouth opened and he began to start speaking "Alec you are seriously messed up. Come get in this bed now. We need to talk about this."

I got into bed with Elliot and he had his arms out waiting for me. It wasn't weird he did that. When we were having a heart to heart, he or I would give the other a hug to show some affection towards the other. He is like my brother. I love him. Elliot knows a lot of detailed things about me. I know I can trust him, I've known him for such a long time, that now he's become the person that I feel he would lay his life down for me. That is the kind of person I need in my life! Not someone that throws it straight back in my face.

So the night progressed as Elliot and I discussed the matter at hand. I admitted that I find Cole attractive; he wasn't shocked. 'He is a good looking guy' I said to him. I wasn't sure why I was feeling like this, and it was wrong for me to feel like this. He replied with; "people feel attracted to people for unknown reasons, sometimes. There isn't a right, or wrong in that area. People feel things for people that aren't always the best, but you have to deal with it in your own way. Yes it may be hard but having known you for so long I know you will do the right thing, by yourself. You know me Alec. I'm not going to judge you. I'm just glad you're finally being your own person." Elliot always knows the right things to say when I'm on the verge of a break down. They have become more regular since Alexis and I have broken up. But this, he was wrong. I cannot accept that having feelings for Cole is the right thing for me. I won't let anyone tell me any differently, because only I know what it right for me, and it's certainly not Cole Jameson.

"The whole situation with Cole…" I waited for him to make sure he was listening. He nodded to state he was. So I continued. "Well, there isn't going to be a problem with that. Not at all. You see, even though I do feel attracted to him. It is wrong. I cannot grasp what I would do if I were to be put in a sexual situation with him. I know it would be impossible. For me anyway. I cannot put myself into that type of situation. It would bring so many scars back to life. I know I not be able to handle them." I stopped as I realised I was babbling. "Sorry I was babbling." I shrugged sympathetically

Elliot didn't say anything at first. He was gathering his thoughts. "I don't think you were babbling. You were being truthful. If you think that he would push you that far, then you should stay away from him." Elliot looked at me questionably. I knew the full meaning behind those lines. He knew Cole wouldn't do that, but one can never be sure. I'm not putting myself in that situation. 'No way! Not in a million years'!

"I don't know if he would. But if you were in my situation, what would you do?" I only asked because I want his opinion. I can then decide what to do then. I know I have to do the right thing by me.

"Well for starters if Cole Jameson was hitting on me, I would not be hesitating." Elliot said. Raising his eyebrows. "But given your past, I don't blame you for being so cautious."

"Dude, are you turning gay on me now?" I knew he was messing.

"Well Alec, are you turning gay on me now?" Elliot said turning my own question around to me, while pinching my nipple. That hurt!

"No I am not. I just think he's hot that is it! I'm aloud to appreciate a guy aren't I?" I knew Elliot would be shocked by my outburst but it was true. When Alexis and I were out in town I could easily say to her when we saw a good-looking guy; "He's a good looking guy." And she would comment back saying; "Hell yeah!" it was just a natural thing to me. However, now with Cole being more than a good looking guy. That scares me. I'm not going to elaborate on the matter any further. It was time I began to discuss the whole; save Alec scheme! I need to be myself, not someone living behind a charade. "Anyway, I need to be a person that can decide in his own life choices, without anyone else. How shall I begin?" I asked Elliot because I knew he would come up with the best answer. He knows how I think; he knows how I work as a person, better than myself, at times.

"Well you could have fooled me. It seems to me like you're really in to him." Elliot said it in a joking way, I hope. I noticed as I glanced at Elliot, there was something worrying him. I can always tell when there was something wrong with him, because when we tried to hide something from me, his nose would flare. "I think you should do what you want to do for a change, you always ask me. Alec its time you start thinking for yourself, come on you can do it." He was right I know I should, but how?

Elliot's expression deepened. I began to ask why. "Elliot what is it? Something's wrong." I lifted my eye- brows. I wanted to know what was going on inside his head.

"Nothing. It's nothing." His voice was hesitant. Why would he want to find something from me? We never keep anything from each other, why now? It must be something so big, that he didn't want to tell me.

I pressed on. "Elliot, how long have you known me? You can trust me, I swear. I not say anything, I swear on my own life."

"Alec, it's nothing big, it just got me thinking." Now he was scaring me. We told each other everything. Why was he hiding something from me?

"Thinking what exactly? If you don't start speaking I'm going to kick your ass out of my house! Start speaking, bitch -face!" Elliot turned his head towards me, and looked directly into my eyes. I could feel the hesitation in them. Seriously what does he was to keep from me?

"Ok – ok." he repeated. "I'll start talking. But promise me that you won't freak the hell out?"

"Ok. I promise." I said nervously. I pulled my knees up to my chest, and wrapped my arms around to conceal them.

"Right here goes nothing…" He paused for a few seconds before continuing. "Alec, you know when you were in hospital?" He paused to make sure I was sure I understood. I nodded and he continued. "Well, you were still in your coma, at this point. But the night I first came to see you, I saw Cole there. He was in the waiting room. I knew who he was, so I asked one of the nurses why he was there. I'm not going to lie I was a little excited. But I stopped when I came back to reality. But the nurse said that he hasn't left for hours. No one knew why he was there. Don't you think that's a little weird?"

"Yeah but why would that bother me? He was in the same hospital as me, so what?" I glared at him. He got me all hyped up for no reason. I thought this was going to be juicy information. Obviously not! Seriously though, why would Elliot be so concerned about Cole being at the hospital the same time as me? It doesn't make sense.

"Well this is only a guess. But I think he has something to do with you even being at the hospital in the first place. The doctor said that if 'someone' hadn't brought you in when they did..." He paused to blink back tears at the memory. "You would have been dead." I could tell as the words came out of his mouth that he had to push them out. Tears started to flood down his cheeks. "I wouldn't know what to do if I had lost you. You are my brother. Maybe not biologically but to me you are my blood." He said stuttering on his words.

"Why would that have anything to do with the reason Cole was in the same time as me? It's possible that he could have been there for a different reason, I didn't even know him then, you know that. Stop acting crazy." He was making me crazy. But then I began to reflect on what Cole said to me, previously; it clouded my mind. A thousand questions ran through my mind; why would he want to protect me? Why did he want to make safe? Why did he want me to go to America with him? Why couldn't he leave me alone? Why did he want me to trust him so badly? "It all made sense." I said out loud, not meaning to. 'Great one Alec'! My subconscious glared.

Elliot obviously heard me, because he looked at me with a quizzing look. "What do you mean; 'It all makes sense', you figured something out?" I swallowed hard. Great! He heard me!

"Oh nothing, I was just thinking that you were right, we are like brothers more than friends, because we share a bond, so that's why I said it makes sense." I knew he wouldn't believe me; it was Elliot, my best friend. He knows everything good, and bad about me. But the last thing I needed was Elliot knowing that his theory maybe right. When the person with no name, took me to hospital I was on the verge of death, so I have no recollection of the night, other than what happened to me. Still, no one knows the extent to what I actually remember. That will forever be in my own mind. No one else needs to know. It may take up most of my thoughts, but that's ok. Because I would rather live with the bourdon, I can't, and I won't let anyone else for that matter.

With Elliot's facial expression I could tell he knew that I wasn't telling him the truth. He didn't say anything along the lines that he knew I wasn't telling truth though. Elliot knew that, when I was hiding something from him, I would tell him eventually. "Yeah exactly! Were like brothers from another mother!" He said enthusiastically. And the laughter drowned any other thought, how could I think when he was laughing so loudly? So I began to laugh with him. Our laughter mingled into one as we laughed harder and louder. The weight of my thought were slowly disappearing as I let the laughter take over.

There was a knock on the wall and then my mum's voice came louder than Elliot's laughter. "Keep. You're. Voices'. Down!" my mother shouted. We both became silent, as soon as my mother's voice came loud and clear.

Laughter erupted from our chests.

(HAPTER ELEVEN

Three days have passed, and today is the day that Cole goes back to London. The last two days have gone by fast. Working took most of my time up, so I haven't had time to reflect on what I'm going to do with the situation with Cole. I know there is something that isn't quite right. Which makes it more difficult because I know he wants to trust me with his feelings, but how can I do that? I'm not a heartless person, but I'm also not an agony aunt either. So where do I go from here? Cole text me earlier this morning whilst I was asleep at 7am, saying he wanted to see me before he goes back. Elliot has spent more time with him. They have been writing some new tracks for Elliot's album, so I haven't had my best friend either. Elliot wasn't pleased about working with Cole, but Carlson set it up and he couldn't refuse. I wanted to question Cole about being at the hospital at the same time as me. But I couldn't even pluck up the courage to ask him anything or talk to him. My emotions have started to get the better of me again. Every day I build myself up to re-build my life and then it all comes crumbling down again. Alexis was the one person that would keep me mentally alive, she always knew what to do. I know I don't have her anymore. It's been nearly two months since we spoke. She stopped texting three weeks after she told me what happened. "I'll text her later" I said to myself. This is the longest we have gone without speaking to each other. My heart isn't fully healed but I can try and get some closure, maybe talking to her can help me do, just that.

Why does life have to be so complicated? It should be simple. My life is full of dramatics, maybe I could pass on some of it to someone else, and then I wouldn't have all this on my mind. I swear the things that are in my mind should be enough for three other people, let alone, one. It's ok to complain about your life. But the time comes when you have to pick yourself up from your dwelling, and get on with it. So that's what I'm going to do. I'm not going to dwell on the fact that my life has a lot of complications. I am going to work at changing those bad things into good things. It's about time I find myself.

The first on my list is going to be Cole.

So I throw my covers off myself, and get my lazy ass out of bed. Today is the day Alec Robinson finds out who he is, and starts living as the real Alec Robinson, and not someone who got rapped two years ago. I am stronger than I was. It is time to start living. So I plug my Iphone into my DJ system and blast out the playlist – recently added. After the vocal chords of Amelia Lilly blasts through my speakers, I get into the shower and wash away the remaining scars. Well the best I can. I know the memories will never leave my mind, but I can certainly start living my life, the way I want. They may have stolen my true soul, and replaced it with a blank piece of paper, but it's now time for me to write a new chapter in my story. In. My. Life.

After getting myself. Showered, dressed, and something to eat. I pick my phone up. Pressing the homing button, the screen comes to life. I slide the unlocking system, and start typing a message to Cole explaining to pick me up in an hour. When I got out the shower, I could see my refection, but it wasn't me. All I could see was a stranger looking back at me. I hadn't noticed it before, but that person wasn't the person I use to be. I had created a reflection of myself, so that people didn't know the really me. Broken, lonely and scared. That's how I felt, that's who I am.

After a few short minutes my phone sprung to life indicating I had a text message. It was from Cole.

Hey! Finally you text back! I was starting to believe you had gone to the states without me. Ok I'll be leaving soon so wait outside for me. I have a surprise for you.

I text him back as soon as I had finished reading the message.

Ok. We need to talk about something important. I'll wait outside for you. How long are you going to be?

I had to remind myself that it's time for the new Alec to be out and living to his full potential. And then my phone came to life yet again.

I shouldn't be too long. Go outside in like 45 min's! Smiley face.

Forty-five minutes later I head outside to meet Cole. As I stepped outside the heat from the summer sky hit my face. I ran back to my room to get my aviator Ray-Ban's. After finding them in my sock draw, I head back outside to meet Cole. As I put my hand on the handle of the front door the doorbell rang. I opened the door, and Cole stood in the door- way.

"Hey" I said taking note of what he was wearing. A black leather allsainsts jacket, Nike high top trainers, white Zara slim fitting T-shirt, and burgundy coloured slim jeans. After noticing I was making eye contact more with his clothing than eye-to-eye contact. I looked up at him cautiously. He had that smirk on his face; his dimple on his cheeks came in to visual view as the smile became larger.

"Come on, we will be late." Cole said as he turned around. We headed down to his Range-rover sport, seeing this beast under the sun's raise makes its beauty stand out an even more. We got in the car, he placed the key in the ignition, and the engine came to life. I hope he didn't see me staring at him. This is about taking things into my own hands, instead of weaving around them. Its time I stand up for what I believe in. That's to make sure I have people who don't lie to me, in my life. And Cole is one of them. "So have you guessed what the surprise is yet?" Cole Asked enthusiastically. He looked over at me, and then turned his focus back to the road.

There is now way I am going to let this go. When we get to our destination, I am going to ask him the question that's been playing on my mind. There is no way I am losing anymore sleep over this, it's pathetic. I forced my head away from the window so I could look at him, I didn't want to. "Nope, not got a clue." I kept my face expressionless. And turned my head back to look out the window. Seeing the trees go past in a blur, it reminded me how my life had done that. In the last two years, I hadn't given my life much thought, until now.

"Well maybe if I give you a clue, you can guess what it is?" He said enthusiastically, again. Wow! He really is joyful today! He obviously didn't notice my annoyance towards him. What was it with this guy? Ever since I've met him, all he does is make my blood boil whenever I see him.

"No I would rather let my mind run wild with un- answered questions." I said a little too bluntly. When saying that, it gave it two different meanings. I hope he will click on to that when I start interrogating him.

Cole didn't question why I didn't want to know, he carried on driving. During the drive I made no small talk or even look in his direction, he didn't deserve it. He lied to me. Why should I trust someone who is only going to destroy my life, eventually? I am glad I hadn't told him the full extent of what happened; I nearly did at one point. Never. Again. Yet again, I have proven myself wrong, trusting people I thought I could. First it was Toby, Austin and Joel, and then it was Alexis, and now Cole. People need to start seeing someone who won't be a 'push over', but a person who doesn't care about anything or anyone. I'm just waiting for Elliot to let me down; I know the time will come, eventually.

We arrived at a closed - off area around thirty minutes after Cole came and collected me. Cole turned the key in the ignition. And the engine went silent. I took my seat belt off, and got out the car. Opening the door, I could feel the heat radiating on to my face, I took the chance to take off my Hollister cardigan. I stood just outside the passenger door, waiting for Cole to show me this 'surprise'. 'Oh, I can't wait' I thought sarcastically. So as I waited for him to get something out of his car bonnet, I took the time to take a glance at my surroundings. The air was mild; taking a deep breath I could feel the warmth of the summer season. I spun around, trees covered the area we were in, leafs were of a coloured variety. The sun was leaking in the opening of the trees. There were little openings in our surroundings, apart from the road we came up; it was a complete dead - end. Squinting my eyes, I saw a little opening to an un-known area far back in the trees. I wanted to go and see what it was, but I was worried I would get lost. I felt a smile grow on my face. The area felt liberating, and freeing. I could feel my mind wanting to hold on to this place forever. It was hard to be defined. I felt a gush of airflow past my face; my mildly short brown hair was blowing in all directions, pulling it out of its sculptured position. The term people use when they say 'someone has just walked over my grave' came in to my mind. I have felt that feeling before. However, now it felt like I was walking over my own dead self, and bringing the new me to life. This place was a place where I could come and reflect on my life and hopefully new prospects would come to me. 'I will have to come back when I haven't got company' I said to myself.

Turning my body in the direction of Cole, he was watching me. Why was he watching me? His mouth opened indicating he was about to speak. "You are very interesting when you're thinking ya — no." He said, and then broke into laughter. I sent him an unimpressed glare and started walking towards the opening in the trees. "Oh come on Alec, don't be mad. I wasn't looking for long." He started running to catch up with me.

"Well you shouldn't be staring at me, it's rude!" I hated that I could let people know my feelings through my thoughts; with my facial expressions I couldn't lie. I was never good at lying. He didn't reply. "So where is this place?" I asked. I turned to my right, to look at him. He has a backpack on his back. That must have been the item he needed out of his bonnet. I was still waiting for his reply. The sooner we get this over with the better. The reason why I didn't ask him in the car about him knowing about what happened to me was because if I needed distance to run away from him, I could. The thing that played on my mind the most was that he knew and he didn't tell me.

Pulling me out of my internal tirade, Cole began to reply. "It's just over there." He lifted his hand, and waved it in expression to show me where we were heading. I nodded. We were heading to the small opening. As we were walking to the small opening I noticed that the trees were getting larger and larger as we proceed to walk. The trees over hung from both sides of us, the path - way was overly grown with weeds and plants which included; Yellow dandelions, small and large white daisies, butter- cups, green leafed nettles, and other unknown flowery scrubs. It was beautiful. We had to push past them to get by. I lost count of how many times I got stung by nettles. I didn't care. It was perfect. I just wish I was here alone, and not with company. The suns raise came through the trees, brighter than were the car stood. You could see it trying to seek through. It left green coloured patterns of leafs on the soil what we were walking on, the sun was shining through them. I wanted to never leave. I felt at home.

We carried on walking along the bush - ridden path. We got to the opening ten minutes after leaving the car. There was a humongous tree trunk covered in weeds and other plants. Obviously, it had snapped away from its routes, it was closing the entrance to this unknown area. We had to pull ourselves up to get over. The weeds, we had to cling onto, so that we could pull ourselves up. And then we jumped down.

When I finished getting the mud of my camel coloured chinos, I looked around. We were stood in stream of open fields. There wasn't a house for miles, well I couldn't see any at this given moment. The sun was sharing its raise with green filled grass, making it a light green. Clouds were in the sky, leaving patterns of them on the greenery. I was breathless. Cole pulled me out of my admiration. He started to speak. "So what do you think?" I turned my head to look at him; a smile grew on my lips. He was smiling down at me.

Taking oxygen into my lungs, I began to speak. "Well this is pretty perfect to me." I sighed. "I never want to leave." I put my head down, knowing I would have to leave eventually. He placed a hand with a tight grip on my shoulder.

"Well, now you know about this place, you can come back, whenever you want." I could do that, but it would always remind me of Cole. I didn't want that. After today I never want to think of him again, and coming here, I would. The thought that he was adding more memoires in my mind left me thinking why I even came here in the first place.

"Yeah I know, it's just finding the time, I suppose." I lied. We started walking away from the log and walked into the open grass fields. I wasn't sure why he brought me here. But I'm glad he did, even if I didn't want it to be him. As we were walking through the short green grass, there were butterflies and other flying insects roaming around us. I could hear their wings going at such high speed as they flew past my ears. I turned around to look at them as they did. Each time I looked it was a different one, with a mixture of colours. "So why did you bring me here?" I asked out of curiosity.

He answered immediately; "I once flew over here in my helicopter. I saw the beauty of it as soon as I locked my eyes onto it. I came here once before, to make sure my eyes wasn't playing tricks on me. But when I came here, I knew that when I came again I would have to bring a picnic, and a picnic is boring on your own, right?" so he brought me to this indefinable place for a picnic? Well I would never have pictured Cole as a picnic- type – of – guy. We carried on walking along the stream of open felds. Birds were flying above us singing to each other.

"So you bought me here for a picnic?" I asked. I have never once been on a picnic. It just felt weird, yet understandable. This place would be perfect for a picnic. The grass was short enough so that the blanket wouldn't rise to the height of the grass. And there weren't any faeces anywhere in sight. So we could eat without anything making it gross, and uncomfortable. Well uncomfortable could be used in a different term on this occasion.

Cole put his hands in his pocket as we strolled further into the fields of nothingness. "Yeah I did, but I thought we could have a talk about something. That's the main reason why I wanted you to come with me." So Cole has something to talk about. Before he fills my mind with more 'crap' I'm going to go first. I need to know the truth. I know deep down I didn't really want to know.

So I began. "Ok, but I need to ask you something first. It's something that's been playing on my mind for a couple of days now." I looked to the right of me, where Cole was standing. He looked like something was aggravating him. His facial expressions were not lying. He defiantly has something he needs to get off his chest.

He pointed in the direction of a large Oak tree, which looked over a hundred years old. The bark on the tree was shredding away from its body, the branches looked like they were one with the wind; and leafs were falling off the flimsy branches. "Do you want to sit over there? It will be in the shade." I nodded in an agreement. We walked over to the hundred – year - old - tree. Cole took the backpack from his back; he then placed it on the ground in front of us. He pulled out a rather large red picnic blanket and placed it on the ground. I sat down with my back leaning against the tree, as he started to pull out the food.

The food was spread out in between us; I sat there amazed. The amount of food he had stacked away in his backpack was enough for an entire Army, I swear. I picked up a turkey sandwich, which was covered in clean- film. "So this is pretty cool." I hated small talk, but I needed a way to start the talking. So I said the most obvious thing.

"Yeah, I love it out here. It's like heaven." I could agree; this place was defiantly spectacular. He grabbed a sandwich himself, and started to rip the clean- film from it.

"Amen, to that." I started to unwrap my sandwich, and pulled my legs up to my chest. I concealed my leg with my arms. I need to get this over with. "So, I need to ask you a question." He nodded in agreement for me to proceed. "Elliot said that he saw you in the same hospital I was in, two years ago. Why were you there?" I put my head down, not wanting to look in his direction. For the simple fact, if the reason was I, I don't know how I would react.

He gasped, and looked at me puzzled. I looked up at his face. I knew the answer at that moment, but I let him tell me himself. "Why do you ask?" His facial expression became something along the lines of; confused or may be shocked.

"Because, I was in the hospital at the same time. I understand that it could be just coincidence, but I need to know the reason why you was there?" I started to sound annoyed towards the end. I could deal with the truth (maybe), but lying I couldn't deal with.

"You want to know the truth, Alec? Well here it goes..." Cole paused for a moment to gather his thoughts. "I was in the hospital because I was the one who found you, in that god forsaken place." He paused again, his eyes locked on the grass in front of us. Was he being serious? He continued. "I took you to the hospital. And still two years later I can't leave you alone. Ever since that day, I've wanted to make sure you were ok. I saw how bad you were, and I didn't even know you. I couldn't imagine how your family would feel seeing you like that. But the doctors cleaned you up before your family came. I was waiting for them to say you were going to be ok, but they couldn't answer me. So I tried to listen to the doctors telling your family." I couldn't even prepare myself for that. I didn't know the full extent of what he knew, but apparently he knew everything. He still lied; I may understand why he did it, which isn't an excuse. I have wanted to know the person who saved me for so long now, that I thought I would never find he person who saved me. And it was Cole 'friggin' Jameson!

I couldn't look at him, when I spoke it came out barely a whisper. "Why did you lie to me Cole? I thought I could trust you." I may of knew part of what he was going to tell me, I just didn't expect him to be the one whom found me, saved me. He saw me naked on the ground, the night my life was taken from me. I broke into a loud sob; I broke down. Tears began to stream down my face at the realisation it was Cole who saved me, has finally settled in.

"Because I didn't know how to, I mean I was going to tell you, I just didn't know how." He was breathless with fear. Fear, had become my best friend over the past two years. I knew fear and it knew me just as well. His face was full of worry when I finally looked at him. My face began to tighten with anger towards him.

"How dare you!" I spat. "How dare you, Cole! You should have told me!" I shouted louder as the words came out. "You don't understand how long I've wanted to know who saved me" My voice was furious. "I've made myself go crazy over the fact I wouldn't ever know the person who saved me." I breathed heavy. "And it was you all along." I got up from my sitting position and looked down at him with pure disgust; I never want to see him again. He being a liar was an understatement.

"Alec sit down, I will explain everything. And then you can decide if you want me around, after." He looked broken and hurt. Feelings of sympathy were out the door. All I felt towards Cole now were resentment. His hands were down on the grass beside him, like he was holding himself up for support. "I never wanted to hurt you; I just didn't know how to tell you. How could I say; 'oh - hey, btw I'm the one who saved you the night you nearly died." He paused. "How could I hurt you more than you already are? I know you better than you think I do. I have been making sure the best people have dealt with your recovery. Do you know how hard it's been to stay away from you as long as I have!" he started to sound annoyed. "When I found you Alec, I thought you were dead. I didn't even know you, but I knew, somehow that you had people that loved you. So I did what I thought I should do. And that's to make sure you had the best care anyone needed in your position." He looked down towards the ground, like he was scared. "The reason why I know the best people is because I had them deal with my case, which was similar to yours." I gasped in shock. Was he telling me what I think he was telling me? That he had been raped too? "Yes, Alec I was raped too." His head dropped down in defeat. I know how it feels to tell someone something that burns your throat as you push the words out. It's like you're telling the entire world, not just one person. You feel isolated and scared. That took some balls. I stood their shocked, suddenly I felt sympathetic towards, Cole.

CHAPTER TWELVE

Our eyes locked together. Tears were streaming from his eyes, and mine, wetting his tanned cheeks. Cole Jameson was crying, I never thought I would see the day. I felt like I should feel more resentment towards Cole, but the only emotion that came to me was, understanding. If I were in his position, I would have done the same thing. Not in a million years would I want to hurt someone intentionally. And I had done just that. Guilt spread through me, as the thought processed, that I was the one that made him cry. All he wanted was a friend, a friend that could relate to him. I had just thrown it straight back in his face. I need him to understand why I reacted the way I did. I sat down under the hundred-year-old tree, so that my back was yet again leaning against the tree trunk. I was next to Cole, his head had dropped between his brought up legs. I couldn't see the tears anymore, but I could hear him as he let go of his fears. I at least understood that. So I began to explain. "I didn't mean to upset you, mate. You have to understand why I reacted the way I did. It was because; all my life people have lied to me. I never gave them a reason to; they just took the opportunity upon themselves. I suppose I've always been a push over in that respect." I paused, taking a deep, careful breath. "I woke up this morning; I looked in the mirror and saw a reflection of someone that wasn't really there. I'm broken Cole, I have been for the last two years. People, I mean my family and friends have just seen the charade of me, the person I wanted them to see. But that wasn't me, Cole. I can't have people lying to me, it makes the broken part inside me shatter even more than it all ready has. Like I was saying, this morning when I woke up, I woke up with utter determination to regain myself. To be the person I need to be, not the person that is hidden behind fear." I took a large, calming breath to stop myself crying. I had never been this truthful with anyone. Let alone someone I hardly knew. However, this person wasn't just anyone; he was the person that saved my life. A life I wasn't sure if I could live again.

"Alec you don't need to tell me all of this. I understand more than you will ever know. I know what I have done to you; I will make sure it never happens again. I will leave you alone; you will never see me again." He said it with complete determination. Cole looked me straight in the eyes. His eyes were blood shot, his face was tear ridden. Could I just let him walk out of my life? I only had a life because of him. I had always thought Alexis was the one that saved me. Maybe not physically, but mentally she had. Now I realise Cole was the person that truly saved me. I asked for death that night, but god had bought Cole to me for some reason. And everything has a reason to why things happen; well that's what I believe, anyway. With all that into consideration, there was no way I could let him walk out of my life. We both shared the same emotional dysfunction and with that, I needed him as much as he needed me.

Cole sat there, his facial expression blank. "Cole, I'm not going to lie to you, today I had every intention to never see you again after today. However, things change." He looked at me, his face full of shock. I felt the same as the words came out. When I came here with Cole, I never thought I would be saying I still wanted him around. But now I realise I needed him more than ever. He had been through the similar thing as me. And that gave our friendship a deeper meaning than before. I now had someone to relate too. "Things like, I need you, and you need me. That may sound stupid to you, Cole. But to me it means that I now have someone I can talk to, I've never had that. I'm here when you need to talk about anything." I put my head back against the tree. I looked up into the blue, sunny, cloudless sky. I wasn't sure where I would go from here. Today was full of the unexpected. I know deep down that my life needed to change, and its time I start doing things that people wouldn't expect from me, but things I need to do for myself.

Cole brought his head up from between his knees. He looked over in my direction; I straightened my posture, our eyes locked. He began to speak "I've never told anyone." He admitted. His eyes were full of pain, hurt and defeat. How could he never tell anyone? Has he had to deal with all on his own? I couldn't begin to comprehend the pain he must have conflicted upon his self. Having to hold onto something, for how long? I wasn't sure but I needed to find out. "I know if I admitted it to someone it would make it more real, I didn't want that Alec." His eyes started to shed more tears. The pain was radiating away from him I could feel it evaporating. His head fell down between his knees yet again.

I placed my hand on his shoulder; I wanted him to know that he wasn't alone. "It's ok, I understand. You don't need to hide it anymore. You have me." When saying that I wasn't sure what I was truthfully saying. Finding Cole attractive, felt wrong in so many ways, but it was there. Seeing him open his thoughts to me, scared the hell out of me, but it had to be done. There was no way he could have locked that away for much longer. I would be here for him, no matter what. People in general think that when someone has been abused, the physical aftermath is the worse, how wrong are they. The pain that one suffers when going through such violence I don't think anyone can immediately be himself or herself as much as they want to be, it kills you without you even realising it. And for that reason the mental aftermath is far worse than anything physical. Not being able to find yourself is what causes the depression and anxiety.

Cole started to get up from his sitting position, and stood up. He looked at me; tears were still streaming down to his sculptured cheekbones. He held out his shaking hand for me. I took it, and he helped me up. "Come here, man." Cole said. He opened his arms; I gave him a brotherly hug. The type of hug I give to Elliot. A hug of a comforting nature, one that says 'We can get through this.' Cole tightened his arms around me, and I did the same. We both let go.

We began to pack up the picnic. I wasn't ready to leave these beautiful surroundings, but we needed to head back, the time was gaining up on us. It felt like we had been here for half an hour, but when I pulled my phone out of my pocket my phone indicated that we had been here for two hours. After packing everything away into Coles backpack we started to walk back, towards his car. Looking at my surroundings, the sun was still as bright, blazing down onto the greenery. It felt as if I belonged here, to feel free and secure. The beautification of the scenery was outstandingly beautiful. Questions were streaming through my mind, why was he down the alley in the first place? How long ago did it happen to him? Why hadn't he told anyone until now? All these questions remained unanswered.

We walked back to Cole's sexy-ass range rover sport. We had to climb over the humungous log, yet again. My chinos were covered in dirt, Cole's T-shirt ripped on a branch that was sticking out, and it cut his stomach in the process. Thankfully it didn't bleed. So heading back wasn't full of highlights. When we finally got back to the car, Cole pressed a button on his key- ring, and the car lights flashed letting us know it was open. I opened the bonnet for him, so he could place the backpack inside. Cole closed the bonnet door, and then we got into the car. Before setting off he put the radio on, the vocals of Adam Levine came through the speakers, singing daylight. The engine roared to life, and the wheels began to turn.

Half an hour later the time read 4:03 on my Iphone. I still needed to get some answers from Cole. However, today wouldn't be the best of times. We both needed time to get our heads in order, before I start asking him questions. Plus my head is full with so much information that I think if anything else came to life my head would explode. We were five minutes away from my house. I didn't want to go home yet; I was enjoying bobbing my head up and down to the music that was coming from the speakers. The windows were down, my ray-bans were shielding my eyes from the suns raise, and my hair was going wild with the wind. Turning my head from the window and bobbing of my head, I began to ask Cole a question. "What time do you need to get back to London?" A smile grew upon his lips, showing dimples within his cheeks. He looked over towards me, and then turned his head back towards the road in front.

His mouth started to open. "I'm not needed there until tomorrow morning, but I was going to go back to my house tonight around nine. Why?"

I hesitated. "No reason, I was just wondering." I turned my head to look out the window and started bobbing my head to the music, again.

"I don't have to go back until tomorrow morning, really. So if you want to do something tonight that would be ok with me?"

"I think it's best if we go our separate ways for today. Just so we can clear our heads ya- no?" It was the best way for a solution right now. We did need time to gather our thoughts. It's the only way, for now. As much as I didn't want to go home, I needed time to myself, more.

"Yeah I understand. Things are going to change now aren't they?" he sighed. I could tell he felt that he shouldn't have told me. So I pressed on the matter at hand.

"Now you have told me, it's not going to be as bad. You can talk to me whenever you want. Am or Pm hours, anytime." I declared. I moved my head back towards the window, watching the passing trees go by in a blur. Just lately it's become one of my favourite things to do when I'm in a car. I just wish my problems would go by as fast as the trees.

Cole began to speak. "Yeah I know, thank you. It may take me time to get my head around the part that you now know." He paused for a moment. "But I'll tell you this. I craved loneliness, ya- no afterwards, but when I got it, it was like sitting in my own pot of troubles, the loneliness is literally eating me alive. I'm hoping now I've told you it's not going to be so bad." He sighed in defeat.

"I know exactly what you mean by loneliness." I paused to collect my own thoughts. "I think maybe we have different views on loneliness because I have my family, but I can't discuss my problems with them. You don't have anyone; well you haven't trusted anyone to talk to about it. I've had my family to talk to about it, I didn't have a choice, I woke up in hospital and they already knew what had happened. Were as you, you and I obviously had different situations of how it happened. Didn't we? I mean I just presumed." I glanced over in Cole's direction. I didn't want to put myself in a situation were more information would cloud my mind, but in this circumstance that needs to change. He needs help, help I know I might not be able to give, but I will sure as hell try.

Cole flipped his indicators on, signalling left. He slowed, to the point of stopping and turned the key in the ignition. Shutting down the sexy – ass – car. He placed both hands on the stirring wheel in frustration. Oh god I didn't mean to place him in an awaked position. 'Great one, Alec!' He un-gripped the stirring wheel, the blood to his fingers slowly began to flow. Cole turned his head towards my direction, our eyes met. His eyes were full of pain, covered by unshed tears. He opened his mouth to reply. "Like you said previously I think we need time to clear our heads." He paused. He was closing the door to me, would he ever be able to open it again? "Let's not speak about it for a while. Ok? It really freaks me out just thinking about it." I knew from personal experience that pressurising someone to talk about something that they didn't want to, would only push their emotions straight back inside. So the only way to get inside Coles head was to let him be the one to want to tell me. I had to let it go, for now anyway.

CHAPTER THIRTEEN

"Get off me! Now!" I shouted. They were trying to grab me but I wouldn't let them. My feet were faster than theirs this time. I could run, there were no drugs in my system, not this time. My feet was picking up speed as I ran, there was no stopping me now. When I finally hid behind an extremely large truck, I thought this time they couldn't reach me. I was wrong, again.

"Alec wake up! You're going to be late for work!" my mum shouted from the bottom of the stairs, waking me up just at the right time.

I wiped my eyes with my fingers so they would adjust to the morning light. "I'm awake mum!" I shouted back. Yawning, I pushed the covers away from me, sitting up I decided to get out of bed.

Last night Cole dropped me off at my house after we had our little conversation, when I say little, I mean little. There was a lot more that needed to be said. However last night or maybe anytime soon would be too soon. At least I understood the meaning of why he wanted to protect himself. It is nearly impossible to let your guard down, but when you do, it almost immediately goes straight back up. What can I say; it's the result of being so terrified.

There was something always swimming around in my head when I woke up from a nightmare. And that was not having Alexis here to wake me before the nightmare became the over-play of what happened to me. It was strange because my mind would create different places of how and when it happened. Each nightmare was different to the other, never the same. It only got worse with each one. Since Alexis and I have broken up the dreams have intensify. I needed to see Alexis; I know that I could never be with her again, not after she did that to me. But maybe seeing her, just one more time maybe, just maybe I needed some closure.

After getting dressed in my navy shirt, black trousers, back tie and shoes, I was ready for work. Oh and obviously the stylish quiff. When I got down stairs there was a bacon sandwich on the dining room table waiting for me. There was no sign of my mum. "Thanks mum! I shouted because she wasn't insight.

"Alec, there is no need to be shouting ya mouth, I'm right here in ma heaven." Heaven meaning her kitchen, my mum loved to cook. She would enter in the local cake bake contents every year. She never won, but that didn't stop her. She would cook up a storm in that kitchen of hers, and if you got in her way she would use certain riddles such as; I'll be taking that tongue out a your mouth and cooking that in one on a my pies. They never made sense to me, but she said them anyways. "You better hurry up and eat that bacon before it gets cold!" she sounded annoyed.

"Sorry mum I was getting ready." I sat down at the table and started eating away the sandwich. The declivous taste of the bacon lingered on my taste buds as I went to get a drink. "Hey mum". I waited for her attention. She stopped cleaning the pots and I leaned against the counter top of the kitchen. "What do you recon about me meeting up with Alexis today?" I knew she wouldn't approve, but I had to ask her opinion anyway.

"Son, ya make your own choices in life, that's not ma decision to make. That's yours. I'm not saying I'll be happy about it though." See what I mean? She always said the right thing when I needed it. Even though I wouldn't be admitting the main severe thoughts that go through my head. They would creep my mum out, well that's what I told myself, but I know the reason why was because I didn't want her to hurt anymore than she already was. Knowing your son was rapped was enough for her to know, she didn't need to know the defined details of the situation. It would kill her.

"See you later mum." I said walking out the front door. I had my satchel bag that I use for work on my left shoulder, and within the bag I had my notice of resignation for work. Like yesterday I woke up so determined to create a new life for myself, and that is what I plan on doing. You see, when I began working at Topman it was my first job straight after I was able to work again. I owed a lot to that company and the people I worked with; they helped me re-build my confidence, without knowing the reason why. Now I find myself thinking that because I rely on them so much it's holding me back, and with that knowledge I knew the right thing would be to leave. For just under two years I had put my heart and soul into the company, and that helped me find myself again. It was time I moved on. The weird thing is, when I would annoy someone at work, it hurt me. The ridiculous reason for that is, because they helped me create a different life for myself, without even knowing what happened to me. It was crazy to think that I felt more at home at work than at my own house. I wouldn't be coming home again after my notice cleared.

I got on the train around eight fifteen. I pulled my phone out of my pocket as the train began to move. I decided it was time to have a talk with Alexis. So I texted her saying 'Hey, sorry I have been in contact. Would you like to meet up tonight?' I waited for a reply, but there wasn't one. I waited outside work to give her a few more minutes to text back, but still nothing.

Grace "Thanks, my love", let me in the thick glass doors. I gave her wink as I walked past her. Grace has beach blond hair, deep blue eyes, although she was wearing her work uniform, she still looked elegantly polished to perfection, she's wearing rocker style heals with gold studs imprinted in the black material, skinny high waist wet look leggings, white tank –top and a black blazer with gold lining finishing off her outfit. Her perfect olive skin tone was shinning with her sculptured makeup. Grace held the door open for me. Grace and I have been friends throughout my time at Topman, She and I clicked as friends, and it was like knowing her for years, even when we first met. Her quirky personality made me like her straight away. When we first met, instead of giving me a hand- shake, she wrapped her arms around me and introduced herself. It made grace whom she is; she trusts everyone, and puts her heart into everything.

"Hey, sexy. How are ya doing'?" She locked the door behind her and turned her head to look at me. We always give each other pet names. We aren't allowed to do it during opening hours though. A couple of times I made a mistake by calling her 'Gracie baby' over the radio, I got a verbal warning each time. Grace just laughed.

"I'm good sexy leg's, How are you?" I said as we started to walk up the escalators.

"I'm brilliant!" She said enthusiastically, as always. "I still can't stop thinking that Cole Jameson would want to come into a shitty town like Canterbury to come looking for you!" Every day since Cole had gone in, and asked for my mobile number she always said something about him. It drove me crazy, and she knew it did. However, it didn't stop her it just made her do it even more. Each time I would reply with 'He's a 'no body,' get over it' but now I couldn't say that, Cole was my friend, and I was his only friend. He deserved to be thought as a real person, not just a pop star.

"Yeah well I guess he is a cool guy isn't he?" I laughed out loud. I knew it would shock Grace, but I didn't care. I made my way over to my locker. Grace was right behind me. I could tell by her shocked facial expression that she didn't believe me so I pressed on. "He is, honestly"

"What do you mean? I thought you only saw him once? And you don't even like him." she declared, with a questionable look upon her face. I did lie about seeing him all the other times, the only time she knew of was the time after he went to Topman asking for my number. I didn't see the point in telling the world that I knew an international superstar, it still doesn't have any meaning to me, and he is just a normal guy with as many problems as me.

"Well I may have lied about seeing him only once." I admitted. "It was because I didn't want anything to do with him. Plus I have a strict rule to keep my social life away from my working one, you know that." I knew Grace would be mad at me because she always classed me more as a friend than a work colleague. I was right, her eyes grew into a thin line, seeing her mad with me made me feel uncomfortable, I have never seen this side of her. But I had to keep Cole away from my life as much as possible, for my sake as much as his. My life was complicated without having people fascinating over the fact that I knew him. As it turned out he had as many problems as me. For instance, he had to fool the entire world that he withheld such problems, whereas for me it was just a matter of two family members and two friends, he and I are worlds apart.

"You should have told me sooner." She sounded disappointed. "Have I once told anyone something that you told me to keep to myself? No, I have not." She turned on her heels away from me, and walked into the toilets. I deserved that. She was right, as always. I should have trusted her. How could I though? How was I supposed to tell her something that wasn't even anything anyway? I mean, Cole and I wasn't even friends, well I didn't class us as friends. To me there was no point in pointing out something that wasn't even happening.

Customers gathered on the shop floor, it was almost suffocating. They crowded the cash desk; I was working on like a herd of Elephants. I handed in my notice to Rachael at 12 o'clock; her only comment was, 'about time'. She didn't shock me; I predicted that exact comment. I knew she wanted me to leave. That was ok because I know my colleagues would want me to stay. Not that it really mattered, but I would like to think so. When I handed in my notice I told Rachael not to tell anyone until it was too late, I hate goodbyes. I consulted with grace about my decision; she said it was the right thing to do. I knew it was, but that didn't stop the nervous from surfacing. The eight hours of work lengthened as the hours progressed; the time began to slow as the ending of the day became closer. It seems that the last half an hour of each shift always feels the longest. Grace and I spent lunch together at the local Café. She decided to drop her annoyance towards me, when I said I was sorry. They make the best jacket potatoes, at the café. She didn't bring up Cole, once during lunch, but I knew she was dying to know more information. I still didn't let on. But the truth was, I didn't even know the real Cole Jameson, not really. I knew the Cole everyone else knew, or thought they knew. I was dying to know the person behind the charade.

Grace gave me a lift home after work. I got changed into more casual clothes after work, clothes I bought in my workbag. We made our way to the parking lot past Tesco's superstore. "It's this way babe". Grace said as she indicated the location of her car. The black with white strips along the top of the body was in plain sight; her mini copper was in visible view. A tall 6 ft wall surrounded the parking lot with trees hovering above them, red squirrels were coming out on to the tree branches as we furthered to the car, the gravel on the ground made a scrunching sound as I was walking. Just before we get to the car grace pulls out her keys and presses a button and the light on the car flickers indicating it's open.

The left hand passenger side was impossible to get to; it was enclosed between a blue Vauxhall Corsa. "Grace, you're going to have to pull out, there's no way I can get my arse down there." I said. I stood with my workbag in my grasp, at the rear of the mini cooper.

"OK gorgeous, give me a minute." Grace said. I laughed. She opened her car door and jumped in. She turned the engine on and put the car in reverse, I moved away. She pulled the car out of the parking spot.

I opened my door and climbed in. I threw my work- bag in the back of the car, next too graces DKNY barrel bag. She moved the gear stick into 1st and the car began to move forward. It was time to press on to the matter that was on my mind. "I text Alexis earlier, and she still hasn't text back." I waited for grace to either slap me or, shout at me. She never liked Alexis; she never had a reason why. Grace said she just does. I never questioned the reason why; everyone is entitled to his or her own opinion.

"Now, why did you go ahead and do that? Hey?" she said in a stern harsh voice, keeping her eyes on the road as we pulled out of the parking lot.

"I wanted to see her, I guess." I paused. I knew what she was thinking. "I'm not getting back with her if that's was you mean." I focused on the road ahead as I waited for her reply.

She sighed before she replied. "Well Alec you make your decisions on your own. I know that. Sometimes you really do need to see life in a different perspective. What I mean by that is; you need to think before you do something. How do you know that she's not going to mess with your mind, that girl is all kinds of fucked up, I even know that, and I don't know that girl very well." Grace was right, she only met Alexis three times, and that was only on passing in the street. But all I did was talk about Alexis around Grace, I never mentioned a bad word about her, but Grace, She made her own creations of Alexis.

"Yeah I know, babe. But I need to see her. I need to see her, to get some closure from her. It's hard to say without sounding stupid, but I think I need to let myself go, not her." It was true I do need to do just that. I had only just realised, but that is what I need to do. I may want to start a new life, but I need to say goodbye to the life I'm leaving behind, the biggest part is Alexis. I pulled my phone out of my pocket, pressing the homing button the phone came to life. I needed to see her, and I knew where she would be, at work. "Grace I need to go to the Three Tons. Can you drop me off their please?"

"Yeah of course, you know that, was one hell of a speech. I know you need to do that, just please be careful. I would like to see you in one piece, not a thousand." Grace was right again. The place where Alexis worked was, let's just say, it isn't the place where I would normally go. It was a place where the rich went to socialise, I knew I would stick out like a saw thumb, I was classed more of a lower class person, there anyway. That is why I never went. So I went on my messages icon, and started typing. 'I'm coming to see you. Thought I would let you know.' I pressed send.

"I don't even know what I'm going to say to her." It was true. I wanted to see her but I didn't know what to actually say. What do you say to the girl that broke your heart? I haven't got a clue!

"Well how about; just thought I would let you know I'm starting my new life, and I'm saying goodbye, goodbye. And then walk out." Grace laughed out loud, I laughed with her.

I stopped laughing, and sighed. "I'm being series; I don't know what the fuck I'm supposed to say. I don't want to go in there like a blubbering idiot." I said with a sarcastic tone.

Grace looked over at me giving me a sympathetic smile. "When you go in there you will be fine, you will know exactly what to say. Believe me." Could I really believe her? Could I just go in there, and let the words just flow out my mouth? Well it didn't look like I had a choice because nothing was coming into mind. I wish I had one of those little ear bud things were someone could tell me what to say.

"I hope your right because in ten minutes I'm going to be face to face with her." I shivered at the thought. I hadn't seen the girl who had broken my heart, the same girl that helped me regain my strength to continue with my life, for two months nearly. I don't know how we got to this point; I know some how it was my fault because everything was. My heart still ached for her to be in my arms. I want her back so badly, she was my life for such a long length of time, and I thought I wouldn't be able to live without her. But somehow I'm doing it. Although, I'm weak, just being in her presents will crush me, I just know. I wish there was an explanation for everything, but that would make life un-complicated, yeah, like that would ever be possible.

We pulled up outside the Three Tons. "Right, here goes nothing. Wish me luck." I glanced in her direction.

"Good luck, my darling. You will be fine. Do you want me to wait for you?"

"No it's ok, I'll walk home, and it's not that far from here." She nodded in agreement. I spun around in my seat to get my bag from the back seat, and kissed grace on the cheek, making her blush. "Thank you for everything babe." I put my hand on the handle and pulled it to open.

"No problem, ring me later." I nodded. I got out of the car and closed the door behind me. Right, here goes nothing!

CHAPTER FOURTEEN

I slung my workbag over my shoulder and walked to the doors of the restaurant/bar. The building is a new build; the outside was modern, new style red brick held the structure, with flowers hanging in baskets, from the bricks. The thick, wide and large glass doors were shinning in front of me, from the suns raise, two wide balcony style windows on either side of the door, and another two above. I placed my hand on the handle that said push or pull. I pushed. When I pressed the door too open, a familiar laughter came to my ears and the door widened open. Alexis. I knew the laughter more than the location of my house. I could point that laughter out between a hundred different ones. I hadn't heard it in such a long time, my chest tightened. My breathing intake was quickening. I am just a few meters away from the girl I love, I mean loved. 'Oh Alec who you kidding off course you still love her.' I said to myself. But that didn't matter, I need to do what I intend to do. This is to say goodbye.

I placed both feet in the doorway. The inside, is like walking into an overly large hallway. The walls covered in olive green paint, over priced paintings attached to the walls, spotlights covering the ceiling; marble flooring stretched the length of the restaurant and bar, a front desk appearing in front of me as I walked further into the building. The smell of rosemary and lemons entered my nose, the sweet smell was lingering in air, not a bad one, I must say. I felt out of place as soon as I entered. This place looked as elegant like Buckingham palace, and here I am wearing 90's style baby blue jean, white Lacoste high –tops and a black Ralph Lauren top, Yes I most defiantly didn't belong here. I said to myself. The clerk saw me walking toward him, a smirk covered his lips, and he knew me. I instantly knew who he was. His name is James, he is bold headed and a fashionable style of stubble showing on his checks, hazel eyes, and a scar above his eye. He lifted his arm and rolled up his sleeves, showing a full-length tattoo sleeve on either arm. His facial age looked around twenty years old but I know his true age, which Is 25. He and Alexis have worked together for around a year now, he's always flirting with her, and so she said. I don't know what to believe now; maybe it was her who was flirting. I pushed my ego aside, and walked up to James.

"Hey man, I'm looking for Alexis. Can you tell her I'm here please?" I stood my ground; there was no way this guy was getting the better of me. Intimidation was for the weak minded. He didn't know that I was weak so I could play along with the charade.

"Now's a bad time. We are busy dude, sorry, no can do." The smirk showed on his lips again.

I glared at him. "Fine. I'll wait until she finishes. Tell her I'll be at the bar" I walked towards the bar; I didn't wait for his reply. In the bar area it has a chandler above bar, beer pumps were along the edge of the bar from top to bottom, Suede seating with tables were surrounding the bar area and tall suede red bar stools, at the edges of the bar. The bar was basically empty, well apart from two old gentlemen reading there news papers and drinking a beer, they still looked more like they belonged here, I looked out of place, I know it. But I could not leave until I spoke to Alexis.

I text Cole while I was waiting, letting him know what I was doing, he text back saying 'good luck with crazy bitch.' That made me laugh, because that's what he said when I told him she cheated on me. So four beers and a bacon cheese- burger later, which calculated four hours, I heard the familiar sound of high heels clinking against the marble floor heading towards me. I didn't look at her, not yet anyway. "Alec, what are you doing here? I thought you would have got the message, which I didn't want to see you!" she said surprised and annoyed. She knew as much as I did that I hated coming here, and that it must be a good reason if I did. I could tell she obviously didn't want me here.

I didn't reply straight away, I picked up my beer and put the glass to my lips. I put the drink down on the bar; staring straight ahead I began to speak. "To talk to you," I said bluntly. "So were you fucking the clerk as well" I didn't care if it upset her. The girl I knew was gone, she upset me first.

"Don't be ridiculous" she spat. "Answer my question. Why are you here?"

I spun around in my spinning chair and put my elbows against the bar. I glared at her. "Hmm... Let me think? Maybe because I wanted to see the girl I love." I shouted.

"So talk, what's up?" She said. She sat on the chair next to me. She grabbed my beer and put my glass to her lips. 'God I miss them lips'. I said to myself. I shook my head to gather my thoughts, I can't get lost in old memories now.

"I'm here to say goodbye". I paused. Ok that didn't come out right. "I mean, I need to start over, and thought I would say goodbye first." I looked down at my drink, and pulled it to my lips once again.

"Why couldn't you just text me instead?"

"Because I wanted to say it to your face. I at least wanted to say goodbye to your face, I thought you would be happy to see me, obviously not". She didn't want me here; she didn't want to see me at all. The pain came rushing at me at full force.

"Alec you made it clear that you didn't want to see me anymore, and I'm doing the same as you, which is getting on with my life." She said it with utter determination. I think it's time for me to leave.

"You make it sound so easy." And then it dawned on me, she didn't love me the same way I loved her. What a fool I am. And then something else came to life in my mind, something that needed to be asked. "Alexis, would you get back with me? You know, if thing were different?" I needed to know the answer because the answer would clear something up for me.

"No I wouldn't, Alec." There was no hesitation. My question was answered she didn't love me at all. How long was she hiding the way she felt? Was it months? Years? Days? I don't know. I'm glad I came I needed to know this. Even though it hurt like hell to know the truth.

"So how long exactly did you put up with me?" I snarled. I took a drink again.

"Alec I did it because I loved you, not because I had to." she lied. I knew she didn't do it because she loved me. Maybe she did at the beginning but towards the end, no.

"Yeah that's right until you fucked someone else and that person made you feel all new feelings, and told you that I wasn't right for you, bla- bla- bla. I don't care." I got up from my seat and stood just inches away from her face. "I loved you more than anything, and you threw it back in my face, you showed me that trust as to be earned and when it does, make sure you don't trust them completely. Thanks babes, its much appreciated." She slapped me. I stood there frozen.

A familiar voice came into my ears, as it echoed from the walls. "Alec! Get your arse over here, we are going." He shouted. I knew who it was immediately, Cole. I stood there still frozen, Alexis had never hit me before, and I know it was my fault, but still, I didn't expect it. He stalked over to Alexis and I. Alexis stopped the glaring competition and turned to face the voice, to put a face to it. Her breath caught as she realised whom it was. He stood next to me on my right, as I pushed further away from Alexis giving us space. Cole opened his mouth to speak. "Yes I am, Cole fucking Jameson, now if you have had enough of slapping my boyfriend, I'd like him to come with me, you stupid cow." Cole's sculptured face had turned into a deep frown, indicating he was seriously angry. Boyfriend? Huh? What the hell? Alexis sat there opened mouthed, her cheeks reddening.

I stopped starring at Alexis and looked up at Cole. "Cole, what are you doing here? I thought you was in London, I was just texting you." I asked casually. When I text him I thought he was in London, well that was four hours ago, but I did mention I was waiting for her to finish work. This is getting creepy, first he shows up out of nowhere, and second he's calling me his boyfriend, what the hell is that about?

"You text me telling me what you was doing, and I couldn't let you do it on your own. So I just got in my car, and drove down here." A smirk grew upon his lips. Ok even creepier. He said it like it was nothing to drive from London to Selling; it was over an hour away. Was he crazy? Obviously he is!

Alexis gasped, and then started to speak. "Wait". She paused. "Your Cole err...Jameson, how do you know Alec?" Alexis said out of disbelief, that he would of all people be friends with me.

I didn't wait for his reply; I leaned in closer to her and whispered in her ear. "Cole is the one that saved me." I pulled away from her. Her breath caught in her chest, her hand flew up to her mouth, and tears began to fill up her eyes. Alexis of all people knew what it meant for me to find out who it was that saved me, she understood.

"You told her, didn't you?" Cole asked out of disbelief himself. "I thought I made it clear baby cakes when I first walked in?" He answered her previous question, the one I cut up. Cole looked at her with a questionable look; she didn't obviously hear what he said so he made it clear. "Boyfriend, he's my boyfriend." Cole looked at me because I handnt answered his question.

I began to reply. "Yup, I did." I let a small smile grow on my face towards Alexis then at Cole. The smile began to fade; I need to make Alexis aware that I'm not Cole's boyfriend. "Cole...." The words I wanted to form wouldn't come out; I was in too much shock, he told her I was his boyfriend, why would he do that? Cole grabbed my arm, telling me it was time to go before I could deny it.

Alexis was sat on her stool, tears were soaking her cheeks. "But..." she hesitated. "But I thought we could be friends, at least?" She asked.

Cole stopped me from replying "If you think for one second I'm going to let him go near you again, you have another thing coming, young girl. Its Alec's choice not yours!" He declared.

I laughed. "Alexis I told you, the reason why I came was to say goodbye. I'm starting over, I don't know how, but I'm doing it." I paused and looked up at Cole. "Come on lover boy, let's go." I said it to piss Alexis off even more, Cole laughed.

"I would like to say it was nice to meet one of my fans, but you are nothing but a disappointment." Cole said sternly. I couldn't believe he just said that. But Cole, he disliked her for me, not for him. Someone doing something for me other than themselves means a lot to me. I mouthed sorry over at Alexis, I don't know why I did it, but I did. There was no point in telling Cole to say sorry, he makes his own choices, I can't do it for him.

We made our way through the overly large hall way and out the glass doors. "You didn't need to do that." I said to Cole, he was walking beside me with a cheesy grin on his face.

"Yeah, I think I did. I've been waiting to do that for ages." He said enthusiastically. "I still can't get over how she could do that to you."

"Yeah well she did, and now it's all done, and over." I paused for a second. "Why did you call me your boyfriend?" I needed to know. I wasn't comfortable with him saying it; I don't understand why I didn't deny it though. We took a left and walked over towards Cole's car that was parked in the restaurants car park. That beast stuck out like saw thumb, even in a top-end restaurant.

"Well... you're a boy and you're my friend, which means you're my boy-friend. I just made it sound like we were an item, but in realistic terms we aren't. I did it so you wouldn't look like the one who was still trying to get on with life, when she obviously didn't have any problem with that." He said out of disgust towards Alexis. Cole was right I would have looked like the pathetic one, but I didn't want her thinking I had turned gay. Yeah I may find Cole attractive but I didn't want anyone to know, especially Alexis. We got to the car and got in.

"Well I didn't really want her thinking that I'm gay. How do you she won't go to the press and tell them that you're gay? She might do it to get back at me." I glanced over at Cole who was now sitting in the driver's seat next to mine, I threw my bag in the back seat, like I did in Graces car, and he started up the car.

"I didn't think of that, it just kinda came out, ya –no." He paused for a couple of second; he slammed his hands on the stirring wheel. "Why didn't I fucking think?" He shouted. We got to the exiting point of the car park.

"You do like doing that don't you?" he turned his head to look at me; his facial expression told me that he didn't understand what I mean. "I mean you like slamming your hands on your stirring wheel when you're stressed." I laughed. He pulled out the parking lot. "Where do you plan on sleeping tonight?"

I glanced out the window, what seemed to be my favourite thing to do in Cole's car. "Yeah I guess I do." he laughed. "But seriously what do I do? And I haven't made any plans, as of yet."

"Cole, it's not like its true, your straight, it's not like you will be lying. So it doesn't matter just forget about it. You can stop at mine if you want, it cool with me."

He sighed. "Yeah you're right, like always." He paused for a second. "But what about your parents." He said in a shy manner. He was nervous to be in my parent's house, I hated being in a place I didn't know, either.

"My parents are fine with people stopping over. It's not like it happens very often." I laughed out loud. The only person that ever stayed over now was Elliot, and when we were together, Alexis too.

Seeing her tonight made it real that we were no longer together. I defiantly needed to see her. She had proven that she wasn't the same girl I had fallen in love with, she was a complete stranger, in Alexis's body. I still hate talk badly about the girl I love. Or loved whatever, but that girl has completely gone, I have to keep saying it to myself to make it more real than it already is. Seriously what was with the attitude it's not like I cheated on her, I at least deserved some respect for going to see her, right? I don't know but I didn't want that to be the last memory of her, I wanted to be friends, maybe. At least now I can sort my own plans out. I'm going to finish up at work, and take it from there. I've always wanted to write a book about what happened to me, but I don't know if I could write it all down on a piece of paper. I think it would seriously creep me out, I know it's a good thought.

We drove back to my house the walking distance is only ten minutes. However, driving it only took a couple of minutes. I leaned back to get my workbag from the back and opened the door of the car. Cole opened his door at the same time as me, he walked around the bonnet, and it opened as he pressed a button on his key ring. When he had locked the car we walked up my front door, the door was locked so I had to open it. We entered my house at around 11 pm; both my parents were passed out on the sofa. We went straight up stairs to bed, separately.

CHAPTER FIFTEEN

I awoke from my sleeping state to find there was no Cole. Rain was crashing down hard on my bedroom window, my window was slightly open and the rain was threatening to enter. I got up and out of bed, looking down on my bedroom floor where Cole slept, the sleeping bag I placed down there, was now folded up on top of my desk chair. I went over to the window to close it; the smell of rain entered my nose. It was always a welcoming smell, to me anyway. My mum hated the smell. I glanced up into the dull morning sky, thick, large, grey clouds prevented the sun from streaming through them, and rain was crashing down on the ground, making large puddles directly in front of my house. I stayed looking up out of my window for a few more minutes, taking in the smell of the rain. Pulling myself away from the window, I turned around and started to pick up my clothes, which I threw on the floor by the side of my bed, and then put them in my laundry basket, in my en-suit. I went over to my draws and put some clean clothes on. I decided on my white jack wills t-shirt and black jersey shorts. As I made my way to my door, I heard talking coming from down stairs. "What time did ya two get back last night?" my mum asked Cole. I stood at the top of the stairs listening to their conversation.

"I think it was around 11pm, Mrs Robinson." Cole stated. He always called my mum 'Mrs Robinson'. My mum said that it made her feel somewhat eligible to be in the presents of Cole, because of his fame.

"And ma boy is still up in his bed at 10am." She paused. "When that boy gets up am goin' ta tell him what good boy he's been, taking ya in when ya had know where else ta go. I know I did well by ma boy." I heard pots crashing together, my mum loved to make a lot of noise when she was washing pots. I started to creep down the stairs, slowly.

"You most certainly did Mrs R. Alec is the best person I know, he's been a real good friend to me, I honestly don't know what I would do without him."

My mum sniffled. "Oh now don't go ahead and be all soppy like that, ya gunna make a grown women cry." Oh mum, it only takes a sad movie, or a baby being born on one born every minute, to make you cry. She really is a sympathy lover. I didn't think he felt so strongly about our friendship, but he obviously did. I crept down more steps.

I made my way to the bottom of the staircase, not making a sound. Cole continued in the conversation. "Oh I'm sorry Mrs R. I didn't mean to upset you." I have to stop her from making him feel bad. I walked into the kitchen.

My eyes found Cole immediately; he was stood leaning against the kitchen worktop, next to the microwave. Dark brown eyes were staring back at me. His outfit consisted of, jogging bottoms, Nike high-top trainers and a vest top. He was dripping wet; a towel was slung over his muscular shoulders and upper arms. "Good morning sleepy head." Acknowledging me, smiled at me whilst showing his bright white veneer teeth.

My mum spun around to look at me. "Good morning' baby boy." she went over to the kettle and switched it on. "Coffee or hot coco?" She smiled back at me.

"A very large coffee please, mum." I turned my head to look at Cole. "Morning. Why are you up so early, and dripping wet?" I knew he went outside, but I wasn't sure why.

He smiled back at me and looked down at his dampness. "Yeah well, some of us have fitness plans early in the morning. So because you haven't got a gym I had to result in running." He smirked. My mum pulled out a cup from the cupboard.

"Oh – ok. You're crazy. I like keeping fit, but there's a time for that 'shizzle.'" The kettle stopped boiling and she started to pour water in my cup.

"It makes me feel alive. That's why I do it." Cole said. I knew the secrete meaning behind those words. He meant it helps him forget for a while, that's why he feels alive. I understood and he understood me.

I changed the subject. "So what do you want to do today?" I asked. I walked over to my cup of coffee, and put it to my lips. I glanced over at Cole over my cup.

My mum cleared her throat. "Ya two aren't going anywhere!" she declared. I looked at her questionably. "Because ya gunna help me and ya dad paint."

"I didn't even know you were painting mum. Why now?" I really didn't want to stay in. All mum would do is play 80's music really loud, and make a fool of me in front of Cole.

"Because I say so." She stopped, and looked at Cole. "And don't think your gunna get out of this. Your gunna help too, young man." Cole was open eyed shocked. When my mum had made plans for you, there was no way to get out of them. Even on death road, if my mum had plans for you to do something for her, I wouldn't be surprised if she did mouth –to – mouth, just so you could do it first!

"Yes Mrs Robinson, of course." He seemed more scared than I did. It didn't surprise me; my mum is pretty scary! Cole looked at me, I think for help. I laughed at his nervousness.

I stopped laughing at Cole and turned my head to look at mum who was now going into the living room. "Mum don't go scaring my friends away. He isn't going to want to come back if you scare him. And what do you even want us to paint?"

"I'm not scaring the boy. I'm just making it clear that he's gotta help ya. Ya can do ma hallway. Me and ya dad are gunna be out for a lil while, and ya will need as much help as ya can get." She laughed. "It's a good job Cole's got his muscles to keep up with ya." My mum said. She carried on walking towards the living- room. The reason why mum said to keep up with me was because, when I paint, it kind of becomes an obsession to get it done within a day, no matter the size of the room. A little pathetic I know. In the last two years, I have painted my room at least twenty times; it takes my thoughts away when I have to concentrate. Plus, I get a new room feeling.

"Alec its fine. I don't mind honestly." Cole said. I wasn't sure if he was just being nice or being very good at hiding the fact he didn't want to, because he had a real big smile upon his face.

"Ok… as long as you're sure." I looked at him with a look to say, you better be sure. If he thought that run, this morning was a good exercise, he had another thing coming. "Don't worry it not take us long". I whispered to Cole.

"Wait. I don't have anything to wear." Cole said.

My mum's voice rose high. "Alec, go get that boy some of ya scrubs!" she shouted. Ha! Not getting out of it that easy!

I went up stairs and did exactly what my mum said. I grabbed Cole some of my old black jogging bottoms and a old red t-shirt I don't wear anymore, I also chose out some clothes for me which consisted of; Old blue denim shorts and a tank top. Whilst I was up stairs I brushed my teeth and put on the clothes I got out. Cole came up stairs and got his clothes, after I brushed my teeth. He then went into my en-suit and got changed into the clothes I set out for him. It was a weird feeling having someone who I don't really know in my house, but it didn't feeling uncomfortable. That scared me the most. Yes Cole and I share similar pasts, but that doesn't change the fact that he could still hurt me. If I trusted him, just a little, I could get hurt again.

After Cole got changed we made our way out to the garage to gather all the equipment we will need. When we got down there I forgot how messy it was, I felt automatically embarrassed. Cole didn't even acknowledge the messiness; I was slightly delighted. Cardboard boxes were scattered everywhere all over the floor. The garage was mainly used as a storage place, my mum's storage place. When my mum would go out shopping, she would always, and I mean always come back with double or triple of everything. Her excuse was, you never know when the deals are gunna change. But it didn't matter how much my dad and I would protest against it, she would always win, so we just gave in. We dug through the boxes, and twenty minutes and three cobwebs later; we managed to find the paint. Cole was more of a girl than I thought, he shrieked away from them like a teenage girl. I laughed out loud at his screams. When we pulled out the boxes full of paint, they were located in the middle of the garage. I thought up a plan when we were looked for the boxes. The plan was to see if Cole would open up a little, just enough to see the real him. I had a feeling it was going to be that simple, but I had to know more.

We finally made it back inside with lavender colour paint, and white for the skirting boards. When I do a job I do it properly. My mum and dad had gone out when we got back inside. Cole looked at me like hadn't done it before; I smiled at his nakedness of painting. We got everything set up correctly, four brushes and two rollers. It turned out he knew nothing about painting walls; he tried painting the walls with a paintbrush, instead of the roller, what a fool. I couldn't stop laughing, the realisation that he didn't know how to do it, was too much.

Two hours into painting, let's just say Cole wasn't looking white anymore, more like a lavender colour. I have no idea how he got so covered in paint, but he obviously found a way to do it. His clothes were covered; he even had paint in his dark brown hair. I glanced back at my masterpiece, and continued to paint. All the furniture in the hallway was covered in old white bed sheets; they were also slowly turning a shade of lavender. Cole went over to rub more paint on his roller, at first he was rolling the roller through the paint tray and not even whipping it off, so yes it went everywhere! But this time he placed it down and got back up, without picking it up again. He turned his head to look at me. A lavender coloured face with white veneers were smiling back at me, I smiled back. He opened his mouth showing he was about to speak. "So do you think we could grab some food?" He asked.

"Yeah, of course." I placed my roller next to his in the paint tray, and stood up. "What would you like?" I looked around at him.

"What have you got?" I smiled at him.

"This is my mum's house, so most likely anything you fancy."

"Well in that case ill have peanut butter sandwiches, please?"

"Erm... I'll go and check, one second." I went into the kitchen and looked through the cupboards, I was right to presume my mum had everything, I found the peanut butter. "I've got it," I shouted. I spun around a little too quickly and crashed into Cole.

"Whoa, be careful, where was it?" Cole was inches away from my face. Feeling uncomfortable was an understatement; my body began to shiver.

"Erm..." I couldn't form the words. He backed away from me, leaving a divine sweaty deodorant scent behind with him. "Oh... it was just up in the shoulders. I mean cupboards." What was happening to me? I bad become a stuttering fool within seconds. Alec, man the fuck up! My subconscious glared.

As he backed away from me, he walked backwards. We didn't break eye contact. "Oh cool" He said nervously.

I had to change the subject, quickly. So I did. "So... what is peanut butter sandwiches like, then?" I asked curiously.

"You're telling me you haven't ever, ever, tried them?" He looked like he was going to go into shock at any given moment.

"Nope, never." I walked over to the fridge to collect the butter; I took it out and placed on the kitchen counter top.

"Well you haven't lived until you've tried this!" he said it with determination in his voice, his eyes wide.

"Ok. I shall try it, you know just so I can live." I laughed and he laughed with me. It was a crappy joke but it made him laugh.

"Yeah I wouldn't want you dying on me now, would I?" He laughed at his remark, but I didn't. I did nearly die, and he was the one that saved me. How could I not think that a remark like that wouldn't bring up bad memories?

He noticed I wasn't laughing with him, and he stopped. "Oh Alec, I'm so sorry I didn't think…" with my head down, I held up my hand to stop him from continuing.

After he stopped, I began to start. "No it's ok, honestly."

"Come here." He said. He walked over to me and put his sweaty arms around me. I felt a bizarre feeling rush over me, a feeling I couldn't comprehend, and I felt safe. "You are safe," He pointed out my own feelings. His grip tightened around me, I placed my head on his shoulder, and I closed my eyes.

CHAPTER SIXTEEN

"You can let go now." I said. He had clung on to me for at least five minutes. As much as I liked him holding me, I know I had to get the feelings back in my waist. I swear the blood in my body had seized to a Holt. I didn't like the feeling that I like him telling me I was safe, because I believed it, and that scared me the most. What was he doing to me? I'm straight, yet I find him attractive. I've never once found another guy this attractive, was it because he is Cole Jameson, the most talked about pop star of the decade? I'm not sure, but there is no way I'm going to find out, I just can't do that to myself.

"Oh sorry." He let go of me and his face began to turn a shade of red, indicating he was embarrassed. He turned away from me and leaned against the kitchen worktop.

When I finished making our sandwiches, we sat down at the dining room table, and we sat at opposite ends. Cole's facial expression was showing that he was thinking hard, he had a frown above his eyebrows, and his lips were twitching. Just when I thought it could be good to speak about the unanswered questions, Cole began to speak. "So would it be ok if I talked to you about, you know what?" you know what — meaning him being raped. I understood that term because I used similar ones to counteract around the actual 'word.'

"Yeah, I'll listen and you talk, ok?" I glanced up at him, waiting for him to continue, he had his head down. There wasn't anything worse than telling someone what happened to you, and they would buy into the information you were sharing.

"Well… this is gunna be real hard to just spill it out, but I'll do my best." I nodded in agreement. And he continued, with sadness in his expression. "The time it happened to me wasn't like yours." He paused. "I was in high school; I had trainin' on the pitch. When we had finished trainin." He paused. This was hard for him, I could tell. His face was full of fear and pain, it was like seeing me in mirror, I wanted to tell him to stop but I wasn't sure if he would get the confidence to confide in me again, so I just stayed quiet. "We went into the locker room to get changed, but before I could, coach called me in to his office." He paused again. "He said that I hadn't been showing good performance on the field. He started saying things like; I'm going to fail school, I'm going to ruin my life. Things like that." He collected his thoughts before continuing. "He said that that he had an idea, to help me. He said to go around to his house so we could go over some ideas. And I went around late at night." He looked up at me, our eyes met. He continued. "He gave me a glass of straight whisky, and told me to down it. I did, and the next thing happened so quickly. I started to feel faint and cold sweats started to pour through my skin, I went really light headed and passed out. The next thing I remember is waking up in my own bed, and my mom and dada were shouting at each other. Saying that I was out of my face drunk and that the coach found me lying on the ground unconscious. I didn't know what happened until I went and got in the shower." He paused. His face dropped down, tears were forming within his eyes. "When I pulled down my underpants, there was a piece of paper in them. I looked down at the written handwriting, it said; you've proven you're adequate for the team, thank you for the big surprise." Tears were streaming from his eyes at full force; his chin was shaking uncontrollably as the cries of pain continued.

"Cole. Stop." I couldn't let him continue. This was hard for me to hear, I couldn't begin to comprehend how it must have felt to tell his story. I never really went into details to what happened to me, to anyone. I couldn't begin to explain, but he found a way to tell me. "Please don't continue, I've heard enough. You don't have to tell me anything else. I know this is hard for you, so stop." I said sympathetically. It was weird to feel sympathetic towards someone, but I knew Cole needed someone. I was that person, not someone else, me. I felt generally proud that he could confide in me. He has more balls than I could ever have. To tell someone your story was the scariest things I had to ever do.

The tears were still coming; he carried on anyway. "I never went back to school. I dropped out the day after." He declared, through sniffles.

"So you never got your GCSE's? I mean High school diploma?" I corrected myself. I forgot his educational qualifications where different to England.

Cole whipped his tears away from his tear soaked cheeks, with his hand. The tears were slowing. "Yeah I did, I did home schooling, trust me, and it wasn't easy to persuade my mom and dada to help me. They thought I was throwing my life away. But then I found music, I wrote, I produced and sang my own songs. That's why Sony signed me; they said I had a new musical talent that needed to be heard. That's when I met Carlson, he helped me with getting my name out there, he even organised the tours for me. That man, I swear was sent from the angles to me." He was blabbering on, but I didn't care. It was nice to learn more about Cole, and his life.

"Weren't you scared about everything coming out?" I asked.

"That wouldn't ever happen. Alec, I never told anyone, I went to a councillor but I never told her what happened. That news would be a first page spread; I could not deal with that. And I knew the coach wouldn't tell anyone. So I just progressed in the music industry. As much as I love football I could never go back. He took that away from me. I can't even watch the sport, my entire life revolved around that sport, to feel like you can't play anymore, do you know how hard that is?." We both shared being so scared of doing something that it scared the life out of you. Mine was to leave the house without someone, and Coles was, in the English term rugby, also known as American football. It scared me that we have so much in common. With mine though, I had no choice but to leave the house on my own. When I first started leaving the house, after doctor's permission, Alexis or Elliot had to walk me to and from places. I hated having to rely on them, but I was just so scared to face the world alone. The neighbours must have thought someone was being murdered, because when my mum would make me go to job interviews, alone, I would scream and shout at her. Now I feel so dumb, it turned out I could leave the house as long as I had other people around me, so that if I was in danger, I could shout and someone could help me. I wouldn't ever go out if the outside of my house clear. I still don't.

"I know how that feels, ya no, to be so scared of doing something that your insides turn. But the difference between us Cole is you never had anyone and I did, but now you do." I smiled at him to let him know I was being the friend he needed. I am the friend that could relate to him. The truth is; I need him as much as he needs me. Because even though I have people to talk to, I can't discuss the things I actually need to talk about.

"Well it looks like we are just as fucked up as each other then." He laughed. I laughed with him. We are just as fucked up as each other, it's kind of crazy to think that Cole Jameson is the person that could help me, but I don't want to rely on him. I know I couldn't deal with the fact that my trust could be broken, I don't think I could live through it again. It would kill the little self-esteem I have left, if any at all. Cole leaned his elbows on the table, and he looked straight into my eyes. "Come with me." he said randomly.

"Where?" I asked curiously. What was he on about?

"Come back to the states with me." He said with determination, to change my mind. He knew I didn't want to go. Could I do that?

"I don't know Cole. Let me think about it a little longer." I do want to go; it scares me shitless that I would even think about going with him.

"Like I said before, you can take as much time as you want. I'm leaving in two months, so let me know before then." He picked up his glass of milk I made when I made our sandwiches and put it to his lips.

"Yeah I will." I picked up mine, and drank.

"Ok, so what's stopping you?" He asked casually.

"Nothing. It's just I don't know if I could leave my family. I don't even like leaving the house without them. Plus I haven't ever left England without them." I said honestly. It was true I haven't ever left England without them.

"Well I have an IPad you could Skype with them, all the time, it will be like they are in the room with you." He really isn't going to let this go, is he?

"I'll think about it." I said sternly. I didn't like the fact that someone was making me do something I wasn't sure about. 'Alec, stop being overdramatic, of course you want to go!' My subconscious said.

"The moments you want to go home ill take you." He pressed.

"Why do you want me to go with you so badly?" I needed to know, before I made my decision. Why would he want me to go with him? He hardly knows me, and what would I do? I don't have any money, apart from my savings, but that's for a house, there would be no way my mum would let me use it to go over there! I might as well sell a lung. There is no way I'm scrounging off of him; I need my own independence.

"Why wouldn't I? I need you there with me. I need to feel human again, Am only myself when I'm around you. I even have to hide behind a charade in front of my own parents. I need you, Alec, please?" He begged. How was I supposed to say no to that? He even had puppy dog eyes; I really should go. Should I?

"Fine! I'll go with you! But you're asking my mum." I gave in. I can't wait for him to ask my mum if he could take her baby away from her, she would cry, she would shout, all hell will break loose!

"Really?" He was shocked.

"Yes, really, but you're asking my mum."

"Yeah, yeah of course, I will. Alec, you don't know what this means to me."

"How do you expect me to live without money? There is no way I'm living off your fortune, I need some self pride." I said.

"You can work for me, I'll pay you. You could be my assistant, mine is going on sceptical in a couple of months, so I have an opening, or whatever you want to do, you can live in my house, I even have a pool, you can meet rocky." He said a little too enthusiastically. He really does want me to go with him. But the only person that could help me make my ultimate decision is Elliot; he is my go- to – person when I'm in need of advice. He is my brother from another mother, after all.

"Are you sure?" I leaned closer on the table and looked directly into his eyes. "Cole, I want you to be one hundred percent sure about this."

He leaned closer on the table. "Alec, I haven't been this sure of anything in my entire life. I want you with me, I'll do anything." his eyes were honest.

"I need to talk to Elliot first, so let me talk to him before you ask my mum, is that ok?" I didn't want to seem like I couldn't think for myself, All I wanted was reassurance, but I knew Cole wouldn't think of it like that. He would think I couldn't think for myself.

"Fine." He said sharply.

"Cole, I do want to go, I really do. But I can't just up and leave because I want to; I have to think realistically before I leave. I'm going to go with you but I need some reassurance that I am doing the right thing. Please understand." My face looked wounded, all I wanted was to make everyone happy, I hate making people think badly of me. I wish it were just simple to up and leave with a click of a finger, but it's not, life is never that simple. I have wanted to leave for so long, that it's become my daydream every day. But I can't just think about myself, I have to think of my family too. Cole didn't understand that. How could he? He's never had the relationship I have with my parents. There is no point in telling him I'm scared of being away from my parents; I would sound like a complete baby.

"Ok just please promise me, in the end you will make the final decision, because you want to, not because someone else wants you to?"

"I promise." I said without hesitation. That is something I can promise, I know I can do that. I only ever say 'I promise' when I know deep down, I can keep it. A promise made, is a promise to be kept- that's what believe. Promises from my dad, are never kept. He uses the word promise as if it is a normal word, but it has so much deeper meaning. It means you commit to doing something, and you won't stop until that promise is made. My dad uses the word promise as if it's nothing, and he breaks them every time. I thought eventually he would for once keep just one, but no, he still chooses to make, and break them. He would say; Alec, I promise I'm going to take you swimming on Saturday, Alec, I promise I'm going to take you to watch England play, Alec I promise to get you a bike for Christmas. All of them were just words to my dad, they never meant anything; to me they meant everything. He would build my hopes up with promises, and then crush them by not doing them. I wasn't about to do that to Cole, or anyone for that matter. Cole still needed to tell me how he knew where I was when he saved me, tomorrow maybe.

We finished eating our sandwich's, and went back to finish off painting the hallway. We completed the painting task my mum asked of us, four hours later. Cole looked generally tired by the end, I would have thought all of that performing and work out sessions would pay him back, but nope this was hard work for pop –star- boy. Cole was covered head to toe in lavender and white paint, by the end. I asked him whilst we were painting what his plans were about going back to London, he explained that he didn't have to get back for a few more days, maybe a week. At that point my mum walked in and over heard Cole, she told Cole that he isn't going to sleep any other place than in our house, Cole didn't argue. I think the devil wouldn't even argue with my mum, so Cole had to keep his mouth shut. I felt a little uncomfortable that Cole would be staying in my house, with me, but strangely I felt safe.

I still had to finish off my notice at work; luckily I didn't have to complete the full month though. I got offered two choices, and they were; to get paid for my holidays, and time due, and the other to take them instead of completing my notice, I took the second option. So with my holidays and time due being used up, I only had three days left to work. I suddenly felt a surge of thankfulness overcome me. I knew Rachael wouldn't be able to keep her mouth shut about me leaving, so leaving gave people little time to hear about my departure. Unfortunately, that still left Cole here without me. I explained this to my mum but she said; 'nonsense, the boy can stay with me!' I again didn't argue with my mum, I knew better. My mum is a housewife, my dad is the one that worked whilst my mum stayed at home and cleaned, made dinner and other housewife things. Cole was in for a treat with my mum, let's just say by the end of his time with my mum he will be wanting to run out of the front door, not walk.

My mum made us all dinner; we had stir-fry with chicken. Cole used one of his English 'slang words' to describe my mum's dinner, which was 'lush'. My mum told him not to use such slang words under this house and he corrected himself by saying; 'It's wonderful'. And then he blushed in embarrassment. I laughed out loud. My dad was sat silently throughout the dinner, he believed you shouldn't talk whilst eating your dinner; I wish he believed in promises.

Later that night my mum brought up the single air bed up to my room for Cole. We blew it up with the pump, well I did, and Cole lay on my bed falling asleep. I had to keep throwing pillows at him to keep him awake, he groaned at me, I laughed. After I set up Cole's bed he groggily got in his own bed, and fell asleep to the movie I played on my DVD player. You can't beat transformers, it has the world-renowned beauty, Megan Fox in the movie, and I swear that body should be illegal to have. At least I'm still thinking like a guy, right? I turned the film off when it finished playing. Half an hour later I was still awake, Cole was snoring his head off, I couldn't sleep to save the life of me. I threw a pillow at his face and he shut up, at least he's getting some sleep tonight.

CHAPTER SEVENTEEN

Some people's views on Religion have always baffled me, to the point where I question if there is even a God, and if so why hasn't he already compelled us to hell for our sins? I suppose no one knows the answer to that until the end comes. If being attracted to a guy is a sin, which I know it is, then so be it. I do find Cole attractive, to the point that it scares me. I haven't felt safe in so long, and it's all because of one person. That person could destroy me, if I gave him the chance. It's a scary thought that I find a guy attractive, given what happened to me, but I cannot dismiss the fact. I know he may not feel the same way, but that's ok, I'm not going to pursue my feelings. That reason is because the friendship I have with Cole is much more than a lustful feeling, its friendship bound by unchangeable circumstances. I can't and I wouldn't want to destroy that.

Today is Tuesday, three days had passed since Cole and I was painting my mother's hallway. In the last three days my mum had Cole; cleaning, fixing things, and she even got him to tidy my room! I felt so stupid, her excuse was; the boys stayin' here he can earn his way!' I'm sure Cole could have paid his way, the easy way by paying her some money, but the truth was I think he was actually enjoying himself. Each night I came home, Cole would be helping my mum cook dinner; he even set the table. The thing that surprised me the most was that my mum loved Cole being there with her, she was treating him like he lived there. He never left the house, for obvious reasons, he didn't want to be seen. He said he was using this time as a sort of rehab from fame.

My alarm waked me up fifteen minutes ago. However, I was still wrapped up in bed. I hate waking up to a cold bedroom, when the coldness hits my bare skin, goose bumps appear, which means, I have all of one minute to get dressed, before I jump back in bed and call in sick at work. Cole said it was hard to sleep with pure silence, so he had to listen to the cars going by to help him sleep, I wish I said no now. I heard Cole get up at six o'clock for his morning routeing run, like he did every morning whilst he is staying with me. He said it was a convenient time, for a run because the surrounding neighbours weren't awake at such time. My mum will have to plan a day of loneliness today as Cole is going to London to promote his new album, at a press release. It was nice to actually talk to Cole about himself, and get to know him better. Last night, after dinner, we came up stairs to my room and chilled out, we talked about his music career, and how he translated his feelings into songs. He said that it's a magical feeling when he comes to the end of the song, and then play it to his fans. Over the last week all I have played on my Iphone is Cole's songs, the pronunciation of each word he sang, made me believe them, it was like listening to my feelings through someone else's voice. It is a bizarre feeling that someone can channel my own feelings through his own words. To describe Cole's voice, it was hard to be defined into words, but if I had to combine the voice that had me so entwined with the emotion I felt, and then I would have to say it was a clash between a rocker/ husky style voices but had indie swag to it. Like I said, hard to describe.

Finally, at seven thirty I drag my lazy ass out of bed. I pushed my duvet away from myself, and rushed to get dressed into my work uniform before the cold travelled the full length of my body. I hate Cole, why did he have to go ahead and open the god- dam window? I finished tying my tie and put my shoes on.

When making my down the stairs, Cole was coming up as I was going down. "Hey, good morning.'" He said with a bright veneer smile. Taking in his outfit, it consisted of; jogging bottoms and a tank top.

"Hey!" I said enthusiastically. "Why the hell did you go out like that?" I asked. The weather over the last four days has only become duller by each passing day. When I watched the weather last night, they said it will snow today, I freaked out. When it snows in England, it's like every form of transport, stops. Which means no trains will be running, or they will be delayed.

"Yeah, it's a little cold outside, but once I got running, I was fine." He said smiling.

"I guess. I'm just going to make some breakfast do you want some?" Coles favourite breakfast at the minute is Wheatabix, with butter and sugar, he's obsessed with it. The weird combination came from my Nan; she said that it would put hairs on my chest, when I was younger. When she said that; I started to eat three a day, just so I could have hair on my chest, to be like my dad.

"Yeah you know what I want."

"Do you want two or three, today?" He liked to change between having two or three, I could only handle one in the morning; otherwise I'd be sick.

"I'll have two today, unless you don't want any today?" He started to walk further up the stairs, towards me.

"Are you being serious? You've eaten the lot?" We met halfway, our bodies were inches apart, and I could smell his scent coming away from him. I swallowed the lump that was gathering in my throat.

"Yep!" He said proudly. "You're the one that showed me what I'd been missin'." I could smell his fruitful breath as the words flowed out of his mouth. Oh so it's my fault all the breakfast had gone, when bearing in mind, he ate the majority, I think I'm missing something here.

"Shut up, and go get ready, I'll meet you down stairs." I said smiling at him.

"Ok, see you in two shakes of a dog's tale." He said. With spending time with my mum, he has learnt some of the things my mum would say, it drives me crazy! I continued my journey down the stairs and Cole began to proceed up them.

I made it to the bottom of the stairs, Cole cleared his throat, I looked up the stairs, and he was looking down at me, our eyes locked. "You are the best thing that ever happened to me, do you know that?" Cole stated.

"Nope, I didn't, but I do now. You're not so bad yourself, superman." I laughed out loud, Cole laughed with me.

By the time I had made two cups of coffee, three pieces of Wheatabix, my dad left for work, he said a brief goodbye. My mum was still in bed when I last checked. She had a few Sherries' last night, so there will be no sign of her until at least late morning. Cole was still getting ready for London; he said he was going to come back straight after he had finished with the press release. So I wasn't sure how much he would be taking with him, on Sunday Cole's assistant bought him some clothes over to last him at least a week. He said he wanted to spend as much time as possible away from his house, he said it had become the home of the press. So I understood why he would want to stay here, he had freedom.

When Cole made it down the stairs forty minutes later, he had a change of clothes with him, in case he had to stay in a hotel tonight, he said. I thought about him not being in my house with me, it scared me that I even cared that maybe he wouldn't be here tonight. He sat down with me at the table; we ate our breakfast, and drank our coffee's. We discussed the weather and how it could jeopardise him getting back here, I told him he didn't have to come back tonight, and I lied. I did want him to come back; I want him here, so I can feel safe. It's crazy to think that some random guy could make me feel safe, I hardly know him, yet it feels right. I shuck my head, to get rid of the thoughts. I couldn't think about Cole not being here, I had to focus on work.

I had just put Cole's and my dish in the dishwasher when he came to say goodbye. "Right the cars here; I'll see you later, maybe?" He asked whilst putting a glass of orange juice to his lips, he got himself a few moments ago.

He put the glass down when I began to reply. "Yeah, I'll see you later, maybe." I said with a fake happiness tone. I want him here more than he will ever know.

"Ok well I should be back for six, that's if the weather isn't bad." His expression was blank. Cole picked his bag up from the side of the refrigerator and slung it over his shoulder.

"Yeah ok don't worry if you can't make it, I'll go and see Elliot if you don't." I said with a fake smile. That's exactly what I'll be doing, if he doesn't come back, there isn't a way in hell I'm staying in this house alone, my parents are even out tonight. They are going to my great – great aunts wedding, bearing in minds it's her 5th wedding, all her other husbands died after ten years of marriage to her. All of them died with natural causes, yet the men still keep coming.

Weird I know.

Cole started walking to the front door; before he got there he spun around. He must have felt me staring in his direction. "I'll try my hardest to get back, but if I don't, have a nice time with Elliot."

"Ok I will. I may see you later, or I may not."

"Yeah, ill text you later to let you know what I'm doin'." He opened the door, and walked into the dull morning weather. He didn't look back.

As I opened my front door, I looked up into the morning sky. The clouds were thickening into a dull grey colour, as I make my way to the train station. The coldness of the morning was abnormal. The cold hit my face as I stepped outside; I gasped at the realisation of how cold it was. I put the hood up of my black Super dry jacket, hoping to prevent the wind from freezing my ears. When I stepped outside the train station at Canterbury, snow was now openly falling from the heavens above me. The cold white icicles were elegantly falling onto the ground in front, and on me. The snow was settling onto the ground as I made my way to work. Great! I thought. That would only mean one thing; I will be stranded in Canterbury. I really do hope it clears by the time I finish. And then I had an idea; maybe if I ask grace real nice she will give me a lift home?

I got to work at 9:30. Before I entered into the building I decide to text Elliot, asking him if he will be free tonight. There is no way Cole is getting back tonight. I might as well use up my night with my best friend. I got my phone out my pocket, clicked on the message icon, and typed; 'Hey, can I come over tonight?' After I finished typing I pressed send, and walked into work.

CHAPTER EIGHTEEN

"Alec make sure you hand in your locker key before you leave." Rachael said as I was walking towards the exiting doors. I turned around, and walked over to the till were she was standing, with a smirking expression.

I handed her the locker key what was in hand. "I guess this is better time as any to tell you what a bitch you are, and you are the most degrading person I have ever met, I enjoyed working here until you came here." I glared back at her. Her face suddenly changed from a smirk, to shocked and anger ridden expression. I felt a sudden feeling of liberation come over me; I should have done that a long ti

"How dare you speak to me like that?"

"You haven't got the authorisation to tell me what to do, you aren't my boss any more, Rachael." I declared. I spun around, on the heels of my feet, and once again attempted to make my way to the exiting doors. I opened the doors, and didn't look back.

My time at Topman had finally come to an end. The liberated feeling I felt just moments ago, only intensified as the realisation settled in that I was finally doing what I wanted, not what someone told me to do. When I told my mum I handed in my notice she was actually happy, she said that it was about time I start making my own path. Although not working at top man, I would not be working with grace, it would be something I would have to jeopardise. And the part that hurt the most was, she wasn't able to get into work today, she wasn't there on my last day. I always thought, because I had spent my first day of work with her, I would also spend my last day with her too. She had a good explanation to why she couldn't make it into work; she said that because of the snow, the roads had been closed. Typical England I thought when I heard why she couldn't make it in. She wasn't the only one who couldn't make it in though; we had to work with only five members of staff. It would have only been a major problem if we were busy, yet there was only a hand full of people that entered the store during the opening hours. So taking into consideration that the roads had been closed, I had no doubt that the trains wouldn't be running this bitter cold evening. Walking to the train station, I took in my surroundings. Snow had covered every inch of concrete, and measuring at least eight inches high. The howling noise the wind was creating entered my ears; the coldness of the wind was freezing my face. The snow had stopped hours ago, yet the coldness remained. I pulled the hood of my jacket over my head, to prevent the coldness freezing my neck.

I made it to the station ten minutes after leaving Topman. As I walked up onto the first platform, I looked up at the lit up notice board to see what time my train would be expected. It read; DELAYED. 'At least they were still running,' I thought. I would be able to get home tonight. Instead of waiting on the cold benches outside, I decided it would be best to go into the waiting room. So I made my way over to the stingy, unclean seating area. When I made my way inside, it was full with red nosed people. I closed the door behind me, and took the seat to the left of the room. I remembered I would be alone tonight in the house that held my fears. Elliot had texted me back by the time my lunch came around. He said 'sorry man, I've got to work tonight. But tomorrow I'm free if you want to do something?' I hadn't text him back, because I was frustrated with him. Suddenly, a feeling of guilt started to surface. Elliot wouldn't be able to take my mind off being alone, but I was the one who forgot he worked on weekdays. So I reached for my phone from my pocket, pressing the homing button my phone came to life. Looking at the message Icon I had received a message from Cole stating he would be able to come back tonight. 'I not be alone tonight, thank god!' I thought. Firstly I text Elliot saying, 'No problem mate, yeah that would be cool. Do you mind if Cole comes with me?' I pressed send. I knew he would ask me why, but I was prepared to answer such questions. The truth was; I wasn't sure if he would still be here, but if he is then I don't want him staying on his own. I then clicked back, and went to type Cole a message. I said; that is brilliant! What time will you be back?' I pressed send, once again.

Almost immediately my phone buzzed to life. The text was from Cole.

I'll be back in around 10 mins. What time are you gunna be back?
I text him back as soon as I finished reading the text from him.

I'm not entirely sure. The train is delayed, so I'm uncertain what time I'll make it back. But you're more than welcome to let yourself in. There's a key under the plant pot outside the front door. See you later! Smiley face.

I waited for his reply. However, there wasn't one.

Twenty minutes later, there was a loud, deadening sound coming from outside the waiting room. I grabbed my work back from the side of me. Nervously, I went to look outside. I wasn't the only one who could hear the horrible sound, my fellow unknown waiting passengers came and followed me outside. The sound was worse than any other sound I have ever heard. The trees where swaying uncontrollably, dirt was coming away from its grounded position, with the high winds. The sound was building into a higher pitched tone, people where covering their ears with their hands, others put on their earmuffs. I was stood there in shock at the realisation. 'What the hell is happening?' I thought internally. The waiting passengers gasped in shock, their heads tilted to the sky, I followed their eyes to see what had them so intrigued. From over the railway tracks, a large white and black-stripped Helicopter was hovering over the station. It stayed hovering for a few minutes, and then moved to the road just outside Canterbury station. Heads were transfixed on the helicopter; they started to exit the station to see what was happening. I followed them to the outside. When I made it outside the helicopter was landing in the middle of the road. Whispers were coming from the waiting passengers, they seemed like whispers anyway. The sound was horribly loud; I put my hands over my ears. 'This has got to be the best thing that's ever happened in Canterbury' I internally thought. Because; it was. I tried to think what could level to this standard of events. Nothing came to my mind. The helicopter began its landing, only meters away from me. The blades of the helicopter were going so fast I could barely see them in such fast motion.

After fifteen minutes, the helicopter landed. Shivering, I looked up. I wish I didn't, at that moment. Because, Cole was walking away from the Helicopter, and over to me. People were screaming, gasping, and cursing all at the same time. It was more than obvious that they new Cole. To the right of me there were five schoolgirls crying hysterically, I laughed. I glanced away from the schoolgirls, and looked over in Cole's direction. With a mischievous grin on his face, he made his way over to me. His lips started to part, indicating he was going to speak. "Do you want a lift home?" He said casually, as if he had just got out of his range- rover, not a helicopter. A large smile appeared on my face as I stared at him. I stood there shocked at the realisation that every person, whom was waiting, was all looking at me. He stood right in front of me waiting for me to reply, his face depend into more of a mischievous grin.

Nervously, I began to speak. "Oh ok, yes please." I didn't know what else to say. I tightened the grip I had on my workbag strap with my hand, a sudden feeling of anxiety cursed through me. Everyone was looking at me, I mean us. What do I do? I hate with all my being, to be the centre of attention, and all eyes were on us. With a large amount of eyes on me, I felt as if the entire place was closing in on me, my breathing intake was beginning to increase as I looked around me.

Cole broke me from me nervous internal tirade. "Alec, are you ok?" He was staring at me with a worried expression.

With shivering lips, I began to reply. "Yeah I'm fine, can we go?" I lied. I thought about getting in the helicopter; I have never been scared of flying, I've always enjoyed it. I tried to push away the anxiety swelling inside of me, and push through the exciting thought of me flying.

"Yeah come on, Albert is waiting." I can only assume he meant the driver of the helicopter. Cole reached for my workbag on my shoulder; his scent came though my nose, I shivered with a sudden feeling of safety. I would always be safe when I was with Cole. I told myself, hoping it will remain true. He placed my workbag over his muscular shoulders, and started to walk towards the helicopter. I glanced at the onlookers, and quickly ran to catch up with him. The blades of the helicopter began to start up; the power of them made everything in its path sway uncontrollably, the freezing wind was becoming unbearable.

"Hello Alec it's nice to meet you. I am Mr Jameson's pilot, please make sure the belt around you is tight, it maybe a rough ride." Albert said over the headphones coming into my ears.

Excitement was causing me to over load with adrenaline; my eyes were wide. I had the belt stretched over my shoulders and around my waist; Headphones were sounding my ears with a microphone curved around to my mouth. Cole was sitting next to me with a gigantic smirk on his face, I looked out of the window to see the onlookers waving their hands, we both waved back. I laughed at the realisation of what was happening, I was in a helicopter with one of the most famous people in the world, and he was my friend, a very hot friend. However, that remains unspoken. "Nice to meet you too, Albert." There was no reply. I turned to Cole to ask why he wasn't answering me. "Cole can he hear me?" I asked. Cole laughed and mouthed, 'what?'

"You have to press the button, here let me show you." He pressed a button on the headphones and my voice came over the radio.

"Ahh that's how you do it!" I said dumbly. "Nice to meet you too, Albert." I turned to look at Cole. "You know you could have picked me up in your Range – Rover." I said sending him a glare.

He laughed. "Now where would the fun in that be? I wanted to pick you up in style." His dark brown eyes were staring at me,

"Yeah I'm not complaining but I see those people every day, they get the same train as me." And then I realised I wouldn't be getting that train again. I wasn't sure what kind of public transport I would need to take for my new job. I still haven't thought about what I'm going to do, I just planned on living off my savings. I couldn't believe it at the time, when I told my mum that I was quitting she knew that I wanted to find myself; I think it must have been a mothers instinct. She gave me the details of my savings account, and told me to live my life the way she wanted to do when she was my age.

"Oh well, you shouldn't care what they think. So Mr Unemployed, what are your plans?"

"I'm not entirely sure. I was thinking about writing my story, and see if I can get it published. I don't know; I still need to think."

"Alec that sounds like a brilliant idea!" Cole said enthusiastically. "I have a friend at a publishing house that could help you with all the descriptive writing. Wait, are you sure about this? I mean this will be worldwide news, you do realise that don't you?" Like I said previously, I haven't put much thought into it. However, Cole mentioning that the whole world finding out what happened to me got me a little scared. He noticed me looking uncomfortable. "It doesn't matter, we can do it together. I'll help you as much as you want me too. But I have one request for picking you up in my helicopter." He said with a questionable look on his face.

"Yeah? And what's that then?" I asked casually.

"I want you to write your story, but I want you to do whilst you come with me to the states. And now I know you have no excuses, because for one you don't have a job and two I've already asked your mum and she said it's completely fine." What? Was he being serious? He actually asked my mum? God, he's got balls. A thought came to my mind. When I told my mum about rethinking my life, she was so optimistic about it. I swear she was more excited than me. It all makes sense now. She wants me to go.

"Ok ill do it, not because you want me to, or my mother. I will be doing it because I want to, and that reason only. Do I make myself clear?" I said lifting my eyebrows.

"Yes perfectly. God Alec, That's all I want you to do, I want you to make your own choices, and I would never push you into something I knew you wouldn't want to do."

"I know you wouldn't, and that's the reason why I want to go." But it isn't the only reason.

"Good I'm glad you know that." I turned away from his mesmerising dark brown eyes, and looked out the window of the helicopter.

When Cole and I got back to my house it was a laughable experience to say the least. Cole tripped over the doorframe as we entered through the back door. The helicopter landed in the field behind my house, the grass was covered with whiteness of the snow. The coldness was becoming more and more unbearable as the hours progressed.

We are now sat in my parent free living room, watching television. I am uncertain what the programme is, due to the fact that I'm sitting next to the first guy I have ever had feelings for, and the fact that they are growing stronger by each passing day, is a shivering thought. The fact that he is so determined to get me to go with him, is making me really want to go. However, with my growing feelings how can I be certain that this won't crush me? I guess that is the chance I'm going to have to take. I've made my decision; I'm going to go. Loosing someone that is beginning to have a deep meaning in my life would be more unbearable than the coldness of the outside. Like Elliot said, its time I start thinking for myself, and I am. This is my decision; nobody can stop it, or get in my way. It's defiantly liberating to be in control of my own life for once, I'm finally making my own choices in life.

Looking over at Cole I began to speak. "I'm going to go with you." I said casually.

Coles face lit up with happiness. "You have no idea how much this means to me. To have the one person in my life that I can unconditionally trust, with me." His grin widened across his sculptured cheekbones. He then leaped over from his sitting position, his arms became wide, and they were around me within seconds.

I wrapped my arms around his muscular toned shoulders, tightening my grip. "I guess you're happy then?" I laughed out loud.

"Happy?" He questioned. "Happy?" He repeated. "I am ecstatic with happiness!" He said with enthusiasm. He tightened his grip around my neck.

Cole let go of my neck and stood up brushing off his moment of freakishness. "When do we leave?" I grinned.

"In three weeks? Maybe sooner, it depends on what they have planned for me." He said in a manly tone, dismissing the moment of feminist.

"Yeah that gives me plenty of time to pack my things. My mum already knows, and with Elliot he told me to do whatever I want with my life. So I guess I'm going; there's nothing more to think about."

Cole came and sat down next to me again; he slumped back in the settee. His mouth opened indicating he is about to speak. "Good that's what I like to hear. When would you like to start writing this book then?" He asked casually.

"I suppose when we have settled down and I've sorted my things out over there. I'm not going to rush; I want to think about how I'm going to explain everything. Maybe get some intake of someone else's experience as well; I'm uncertain how to even start." I looked over at Cole hoping he could help.

His deep brown eyes found mine. "You will come up with a brilliant manuscript I just know it." He said with encouragement.

"I hope so." Cole winked at me; I smiled back.

CHAPTER NINETEEN

Waking me up from my sleeping state, my phone was ringing, signaling that I had a call. I reached over to my bedside table to get my phone. I held it in my hands to see who was calling; it was Elliot. "Hey man, how are you?" I asked curiously.

"I'm good mate. I've got a proposition for you." Elliot said.

"Yeah? And what's that?" I questioned, intrigued.

"Well I was talking to my dad about you wanting to start over, and he asked if you would want to work for him as a trainee consultant? I said I would ask you about it."

"Wow that's amazing! Where will I have to work?" I asked with enthusiasm.

"It's in London. So you would have to move there, my dad said it would be part of the contract for him to pay for your living requirements."

"Wait, I can't, as much I want to I've already told Cole I would go with him to the states for a while. Oh I don't know what to do now, that's an amazing opportunity but I can't. I'm sorry man, tell your dad I said thank you anyway." I hesitated.

"That's amazing Alec! You're finally making your own choices, good for you man!" He said enthusiastically. I was expecting questions, not approval.

"You're not mad with me for going with Cole?"

"Are you crazy? Of course not. That's what I want you to do. I'll be coming over to visit; I can't go without seeing my best friend for ages!" He said pointedly.

"Yeah of course!"

"Anyway man I got to go. I've got work to get to so I may see you later."

"Ok mate ill speak to you later." I hung up the phone to Elliot. I'm so glad he was happy about me going over to the states; I don't know what I would of done if he didn't. In fact I do know what I would do; I would still go, because it is something I want to do. It doesn't matter if someone has a problem with it, it's my decision, and it's my life.

With a grumbling noise, Cole woke up. Well I thought he did, but apparently he heard everything. His eyes locked with mine as he turned around to face me from his blow up bed. "I'm feeling pretty good, and a little guilty that you chose me over your best friend ya - no." Cole said, with sadness in his eyes.

"There is no need to feel any guilt; it was my decision, not anyone else's. I would have made the same decision if my entire family and Elliot weren't happy about it, it's my life." I said pointedly.

"Well does that defiantly mean that I have you all to myself then?" He asked sending me a wink, and a smirk.

I rubbed my eyes to wake them. "Yeah I suppose you do." I said with a cheesy grin.

We got up from our beds and made it down stairs by 10 am, my parents were still out. I knew they wouldn't be back until at least mid afternoon, that's how it always was with my great aunts weddings, she made you get up stupidly early just so you can help her gather all the presents from her local community centre where she always held the reception. I told my mum I wasn't going to anymore after the third one.

It was nice to lie in bed and remiss about our lives. I have learned that Cole has a phobia of jellyfish, due to getting stung by one when he was a child. I admitted that my dad was just a persona of a person; he never really talked to me after what happened to me. I have always thought that it was because he felt that I put my fate in danger, he couldn't grip the fact that it happened to me. So we never discussed it. However, I'm not really complaining, but it would have been nice to be asked if I was ok, just once. After I told Cole all of this he was shocked and said I had him to talk to now. And that he would always be there for me whenever I needed him, it wasn't the same though, I needed my dad. I replied with ditto, a word meaning: that you feel the same.

We are now sat at the kitchen table. Cole is eating his three Wheatabix and I am eating only one. Like we have been doing for the past four days. It was an unexplainable feeling to have Cole around me, he makes he feel safe and secure. It sounds stupid that a thirteen stone person of pure muscle would need someone else to feel safe, but it was easily said than done. When it happened to me, yes I was scrawny, but I also had martial arts training behind me. So I could have easily got away if there weren't any drugs in my system. And now even though I have the muscular structure behind me, it wouldn't matter. Monsters like them know exactly how to manipulate people; they rip your soul out in the process, without a care. It makes me sick.

"Hey Alec," Cole waited for my attention. Pulling me out of my internal thoughts.

"Yeah?" I asked.

"I know that after you hear this, you will through me out and never want to see me again." He had sadness to his eyes; it made me scared to know what he wanted to tell me.

"I don't want to know, I can't lose you." I admitted. "Just please keep it to yourself, if you think that, then I can't, and won't listen." I said with a worried expression. I put my Wheatabix back on my plate; I couldn't eat anymore. Just the thought of losing him was a terrifying thought; I honestly don't know what I would do. Cole had become my safe place, a place where I could go to when I needed help.

"I can't let you come with me if you don't know this. I've been up all night thinking it through and the only conclusion I came up with is to tell you." His worried expression deepened across his face, leaving frowning marks on his four head.

"Ok tell me, but I'm not letting you go, I just can't. If it's as bad as you say then we can deal with it, its fine, just tell me." I straightened my posture to indicate a fake confidence. True fully, I was worried to the core of my bones. My facial expression; was expressionless.

"Ok here it goes," he paused to gather his thoughts. "Alec I have feelings for you, and I don't mean friendship based, I mean full on attraction towards you. And I don't know what to do about it, it's scaring me to the point that I don't know if we can be friends because it's messing with my head, I know that I shouldn't have these feelings for any guy, but I do." Did he really admit that he had feelings for me? An over powering surge of emotions surged through my entire body. Happiness is all that matters because I am happy that he actually shares the same feelings as me.

"You mean that, you want to be with me?" I said nervously incase I heard it wrong and my mind was playing tricks on me.

"Yes Alec that is exactly what I mean. I want you to be mine, and announce it to the world. I don't care anymore, I've had enough of being fake to my fans it's about time I do what I want to do, and not because the recording company wants me to, and I've had enough of being a product to them." It seems we have a little more in common than I presumed.

"I feel the same about everything, and you. I want that, I want us." I announced. My eyes were wide with excitement.

"Where do we go from here then?" Cole said sending me his famous smirk; he drank some of his orange juice in front of him.

"I don't want to rush into anything. However, I would like to call you my boyfriend, if that's ok with you?" It most defiantly felt amazing to be honest; I want him and everything that comes with him. Lying wouldn't benefit me; it would only deny me of what I want.

"Yes, I want that too." There was a knock at the door. "Are you expecting someone?" Both our eyes looked in the direction of the front door.

"No, and the only person that ever comes around here is Elliot, and my mum and dad have a key. Elliot's at work so it can't be him." I said with a thinking expression, I couldn't think of who it could be. It could be Margret and Daniel; Elliot's parents, they never come around here though, only on occasions such as birthdays and anniversaries. The knock happened again. I got up from my sitting position at the table.

"I'll come with you." Cole started to get up.

I turned around to look at him. "No it's ok, I got it." I knew he was being protective, it made me smile, a smile that only happened when I was truly happy.

Cole sat back down. "Ok, as long as you're sure."

I went to the door, putting my hand on the door handle, I began to turn the key, the door opened, and flashes came at me with full force. I was blinded by the flashes, people were shouting; is it true? Are you Alec Robinson? Is Cole Jameson here right now? I shut the door dramatically. "Cole!" I shouted.

His feet were banging on the floor as he ran to me. "What's happened?"

"Cameras!" I shouted, stuck for words to say.

"What do you mean cameras?"

"Open the door and find out." I stated. Cole opened the door, men and women were shouting his name asking him questions like; is it true you're gay, is it true you saved someone's life? All the questions were gaining, I couldn't listen anymore and Cole shut the door on their faces without answering any of their questions.

He spun around to face me, "turn the news on." He rushed past me and I followed him into the living room. I found the TV remote; pressing the on button, the TV came to life. I scrolled through the channels until I got to BBC 1; it showed the local news. There was a picture of Cole and I, underneath the picture there was a bulletin saying; Cole Jameson saved a person after a vicious assault and is now in a romantic relationship with this person, this information is from a past romance of Alec Robinson. Cole turned to look at me. "Alec I'm so sorry."

I don't know why he was apologizing it wasn't his fault, the only person that came to my mind was Alexis, I never thought in a million years that she would sink this low. "It wasn't you, it was Alexis." I said pointedly.

"Yeah makes sense, but I was the one to tell her Alec. I should have kept my big mouth shut." He said running his hands over his face. "What shall we do now?" He looked at me questionably.

"Cole, you can't blame yourself, it was HER, not you." I paused to collect my thoughts "I was hoping you would know, the only thing I can think of is to run, but where?" I knew it sounded stupid because there wasn't anywhere Cole could run; we were stuck in this, together. People knew what happened to me, people knew that we are together, maybe not when Alexis thought, but now if we denied the fact, we would be lying. My deepest secretes was known to the world, and only a couple of weeks ago I was worried about telling the one person that saved me. How time can dramatically change, it baffles me.

I turned my head to look into Coles calming dark brown eyes. His mouth opened indicating he is about to speak. "Fine, but it was partly my fault. Unfortunately we can't run; they will follow us, where ever we go." He slumped down in the settee; I sat next to him.

"Well what are our other options then?" I said deepening my look into his eyes.

Nervously, he began to reply. "The only option is to face this, there's no way out. Alec I'm so sorry."

A over powering surge of nerves ran through me. "I don't know if I can do that."

Cole looked deeper into my eyes; he leaned forward. "You trust me, right?" I nodded. "Ok then, you can do this."

Just when I thought my life was over, I came up with a brilliant idea, an idea that I'm not entirely sure about, but it's the only way. "I've got an idea." I said waiting for Cole's attention; he nodded for me to tell him. "How about we just tell the truth," I paused, I grabbed Cole by the shoulders, I stared into his deep brown eyes, I felt safe. "I can do this as long as I've got you." I said it to reassure both of us.

"Are you sure?" He asked, surprised.

"Nope, but I can't think of any other way out of this, do you? Without lying." I clarified.

"I suppose not, but we need to think about this, are you ready to tell everyone your story?"

"No I'm certainly not, but there isn't any other way, is there? Because if there is I will defiantly take that option."

"The only other option is to deny it, but again that would be lying."

"Exactly! And there isn't any way I'm lying. People need to know the damage one creates when they diminish someone's life." I clarified. I have had enough of lying; its time the truth comes out. A person of their justification, being thought of as human beings, is utterly ridiculous. The only thing that results to describe such people is a piece of crap designated on the bottom of my shoe; and the world needs to know that.

"Ok well I need to get hold if my publicist and see how we can go about this." Cole got up from his sitting position next to me and got out his phone, within seconds he was talking to his publicist. He walked into the kitchen, and out of sight.

I would have listened to Cole's conversation, but the fact that I had so many thoughts running through my mind wouldn't let anything else process. Could I really tell my story to the whole world? Am I mentally ready for all of that? No I'm defiantly not, but I really cannot see any other way out of this. My mum and dad would know that their son's life story was public knowledge and the fact that I'm gay, by now. Ugh gay. I never thought I would be that. Well I guess I'm more bisexual due to the fact that I still find females sexually attractive. Maybe Cole is the only exception? He must be, because I don't find any other male attractive. Maybe, just maybe Elliot was right when he said we cannot chose whom we fall for. But a guy, really? That is seriously messed up. Surely my mum and dad would have heard the news by now? If they have, then I'm glad they don't have a mobile phone to contact me right now; I wouldn't know what to say. The scary part is I'm not entirely sure how they will react. But if it comes to the fact that they can't love me for whom I am, then so be it. I will not hide behind a charade forever, I want to be the person who challenges life's unexplainable circumstance, and I will not hide away from them anymore.

Cole came back from the kitchen, he stood directly in front of me; he had determination written across his sculptured tanned face. "Right, so this is the plan; Beth is sending the helicopter now to pick us up, and take us to my pad in France. It's unallocated by the paparazzi, and we will have time to get our heads around what we are going to say, everything we say must be like a script unfortunately, because if we say the wrong thing, just once they will twist our words into something ridiculous."

"It is completely out of the question to go to France, right now anyway. I have too many problems to be resolved before I go anywhere. I cannot leave until I have spoken to my parents. Cole cannot be here when I do such thing, due to the fact; I have to do this alone. Being in the public eye will have to be added to the many problems. I stared up to his standing position, I began to explain. "I can't run away, I thought I could, but I can't. I have to speak to my parents first and make them see from my perspective what I want, they won't understand. I cannot run away from my problems any longer, this situation needs to be rectified before I even think of going anywhere. I'm sorry Cole but ill to meet you in France."

"Cole's facial expression told me he was thinking. "I'm not leaving unless you are coming with me, I'll wait for you whilst you talk to your parents, I'll go out and entertain myself, and when you're ready I'll be waiting. It's out of the question any way, you need security from the 'press' as you call it, and I'm being the one they have to get though first. Alec please, you can't make me go without you." Coles tone was full of worry.

"Will you drop it, I'll be fine. I'm a grown man for god sake; I can fight my own battles." I stated clearly. My mind started to cloud with the thought of Cole saving me, why was he down the alley way in the first place? The question has lingered in my mind for some time now; I couldn't let the question be left unanswered.

"I will not drop it. I know you can, but I'm being here in case it gets out of hand, I'm not leaving you." Cole folded his arms around his chest, and sat up straightening his posture.

He really isn't going to let this go is he? That doesn't matter now, it's the least of my worries, and I need to ask a certain one. "Cole you said that you found me right?" I waited for him to clarify that he knew what I was saying. He nodded for me o continue. "Well...I was just wondering why you where there in the first place, I mean famous people don't walk down stingy alley ways, I assumed."

They do if they over hear a group of guys running away shouting they killed someone, and making blatantly clear, and then I ran in the direction they came from, and found you."

"Really?" I asked surprised.

"Yes really. I have never been so scared in my entire life, I thought you were dead...." Cole stopped in mid speech.

"Well I have been the cause of many of you life changing moments haven't I?" I said trying to lighten the moment.

"You most certainly have Alec Robinson. First you made me think that I found a dead body, and secondly you make me fall in love with you, Oh and might I add that has never before happened, with a guy I mean."

I stood up; I was inches away from his face. "You love me?" I asked disbelieving.

A grin started to appear across his face. "Yes I do." He said with confidence. He placed the palms of his hands onto my face; they were radiating warmth. He kissed me. Speechless, I couldn't comprehend the feelings that I felt as his lips lingered on mine, inhaling deeply, I took in his fruitful scenting breath. Calmness washed over me, I pressed passionately to his lips, we moved rhythmically together. Cole pulled away, leaving me gasping for air; I hadn't realized I wasn't breathing correctly. "Wow! That was better than I imagined." His eyes were dancing with affection.

Breathlessly, staring into his deep brown eyes, I began to reply. "Wow." I said simply. I was speechless. The pure heartfelt emotions that ran through me were dreamlike; I was in heaven, there wasn't any other possible explanation. My lungs were contracting, aching for release; due to losing my breath, but I couldn't let go of him, I didn't want to. His hands began to slip away from my face, did this truly amazing person really want me the way I want him? I began to question. "You really want me?" I asked curiously.

Confused, he stared at me. "You're really going to question my feelings for you? Are you crazy?" he stuck his head.

"No I mean why do you want me? You can have any person in the world."

Cole shuck his head again. "Maybe because you are the only person in this friggin world that I want to actually spend time with and you being extremely hot is a bonus." He smirked, and a mischievous grin appeared upon his face.

"So you only want me for my looks?" I couldn't hide the disappointment on my face.

"No, no, no. You are the first guy I want to be sexually active with. It scares the shit out of me, but I know you and me being together is want I want, I haven't wanted anything so badly in my entire life." He placed his hands on either side of my face again. "You scare the hell out of me Alec, you don't understand the hold you have on me, and you could damage me to the point of no repair." Unshed tears started to swell within my eyes. Is this really happening to me, he feels the same as me, to the point that he wants me in his life unconditionally?

Tears started to run down my face, Cole wiped them away with his thump, he pulled me closer so my head was lying on his muscular chest. When I thought life threw unexplainable circumstances my way, I didn't expect they would come in a package, large enough to fill my life with the opposite to what I thought I needed. I had him, and he has me.

"You're worried about me hurting you?" He looked at me questionably. "I am absolutely out of my mind worried about you hurting me." I stared into his deep brown eyes.

"Let's make a deal. We will never hurt the other each other; obviously the thought is too painful for both of us." He said pointedly.

"That's a deal." I hugged him, and Cole hugged me back. I let go of him not wanting to, my phone came to life indicating I had a phone call, I put my hand in my pocket to retrieve my phone, looking at the home screen; it said Elliot was calling. "Hey man what's up?" I asked.

"Alec have you seen the news? What's going on man?" Elliot asked in a worried tone, I looked at Cole.

"Yes and its all true Mate, Cole was the one that saved me, he and I are together, B

But that was only decided not even an hour ago. Alexis is the one that spilled the news, there's no other person who would come to mind."

"So you and Cole, hey? How did that shit happen?"

"I don't really know myself to be honest, it just kind of did."

"Oh ok, so what are you going to do now?"

"I'm going to tell my parents everything when they get back, in like two hours time, so that gives me time to sort out what I'm going to say."
"Ok, let me know how it goes, will you?"
"Of course I will. Elliot?" I asked
"Yeah?"
"How do you recon they will take the news?"
"Alec, you already know." He clarified. I didn't want to hear those words, although I already knew them. It was time to get prepared, prepared for the unknown.

CHAPTER TWENTY

Within two hours Cole and I had packed most of my things into bags and suitcases. Cole wouldn't leave so I told him to wait upstairs whilst I talk to my parents; I need to do this alone. I'm not sure how they will react but I know my mum will understand, she always will. My dad, I'm not so sure, he is always full of surprises. We had packed as many things as we could because I wasn't sure how long I would be away, but the plan is to go to France and then head over to the states when it's all calmed down a little. But before we do anything we are going to talk in a press conference in London, so we can declare what happened. Cole said that they will try and twist our words around, so taking that into consideration we have to talk through what we are going to say first. I know I will be ok, I the end, because I have to be. I made it down stairs two hours later; I sat watching television whilst I waited for my parents. Cole was still packing my things up stairs for me; he must love me if he wants to do all this for me. I sat nervously waiting.

With the sound of a key in the front door, my mum's voice came through the living room. "Alec, please tell me none of this is true?" My mum asked when she walked through the front door; I froze at the sudden realization that I would have to tell her everything. She and my dad dropped their bags in the hallway and came and sat down on the sofa next to the one I am sat in, they both were staring at me.

When they both sat down I began to reply. "Yes mum, all of it is true." I said, unable to look at them.

"So ya gay?" My dad asked in disgust.

"No dad I'm not gay, I'm not sure what I am, all I know is that I want to be with Cole, and he is the person that saved me, and I love him."

"Just because ya feeling like this don't mean its real baby boy, ya feeling like this because your mind is all jumbled up, I know how much you wanted to find out who it was that saved you, and all that information is clouding your mind. Listen, we will get this sorted. Ya will be normal again, I promise baby." My mum made it sound like she was trying to reassure herself more and me.

"Mother, don't be so over dramatic. I want to be with Cole because I want to be, not for any other reason."

"Well if ya think ya living in this house whilst ya gay, ya are very much mistaken young man. I am not having no gays in this house, and tell that Cole if he steps one foot in this house he might as well sign his own death certificate. No one turns ma son gay, and gets away with it."

I got up from my sitting position, I walked over to where my mum and dad were sat, I folded my arms around my chest, I openly glared at the person that breaks all the promises he made to me, it's time I start sticking up for the one person that will be there for me. With anger building inside of me I began to talk. "IF YOU LAY ONE FINGER ON HIM, I SWEAR TO THE ALMIGHTY LORD I WILL GO TO HELL FOR MURDERING YOU." I spat.

"Alec, don't ya dare speak to ya father like that, I will not have it."

"Oh come on, he's already going to Hell for the sins he's made. First he gets himself raped, and nearly killed and now he wants to be gay. I think he planned it all along, he's just the kinda person to do such thing." He smirked with delight, thinking he knew right. I looked at my mum, I wanted to see what she thought, her face was lined with pure disgust towards my father, and she didn't believe him.

With all the anger for this man, I clenched my fist tightly; I hit my dad right in the face. "Alec what are ya doin! Stop it, stop it!" My mum shouted, but I couldn't stop I unleashed all the hate I had for him, the fact that he would believe I would do such thing, only made me hate him even more, he wasn't my father from that moment, he will never be my dad again. How could he think that? He obviously doesn't know me the way I hoped he did, I thought that he may feel that way but I didn't think it was true, I thought it was just a figment of my imagination, obviously not. All the love I had for my father had just been diminished at that moment, I couldn't stop hitting him.

"Alec stops!" Cole's voice came through the living room; his feet were banging on the stairs as he made his way down them. Cole gripped my arms, and pulled me away from the man who was my father. He spun me around so I was facing him; he put both of his arms around, securing me tightly. I placed my head on his shoulder, tears started to flood down my face as the thought started to process that my dad would believe that. My chest was aching and straining as the tears fell from my tear soaked cheeks, the pain was worse than being raped, my father had just ripped my heart out, he didn't love me, he didn't want me, why would he do this me? Loud sobs were coming from my throat, my legs collapsed from under me; I fell to the ground as Cole sat with me, holding me tightly to his chest. "It's ok, I've got you." Cole said out loud. I looked up at my mum and the reality of it all hit her.

"So ya are gay?" My mum asked believing.

"Yes mother I'm gay." I said loudly

My mum's face was ridden with pure anger as she looked at me and then to my dad, he was lying on the floor with blood coming from his nose. "Get of my house, If ya come back I swear to god I will go to hell myself." said through clenched teeth, towards me. My mum was dismissing me from her life too? The person that I loved more than anything or anyone, the person who brought me into this world, just told me to get out of her life, my heart and lungs began to weaken, I couldn't breathe. My entire life I looked up to both my parents, I had always told myself that when I have children I would be exactly like my parents and the way they bought me up, Their undeniable love for me was laid out for me every day, I wanted that for my children, but not anymore, I don't want to be like them anymore, they weren't parents.

The tears were getting worse, I looked up at Cole, and He knew what I was thinking. "Come on, let's go." Cole started to get up from where we were sat on the floor, he held his hand out for me to grab as he pulled me up. "Run upstairs and grab you're our bags I need to get someone to meet us at the door." His face was ridden with pure sadness for me, I nodded.

I made it to my room; I pushed open my bedroom door for the last time. The bags were scattered on the floor, how was he expecting me to carry all of these down all on my own, was he crazy? I went and sat on the end of my bed; I looked at my plain white walls and looked at the things I would be leaving behind. Tears started to escape again; I placed my hands on to my face, why are they doing this to me? Had I done wrong by doing what I wanted to do with my life? Were they punishing me for being me? Surely I didn't deserve such hate, I have no family now, and all I have is the person I love and my best friend. I shuck my head, I need to regain myself. I started to grab my bags when a large six foot tall bold headed Aston came to my door way. "Hello Mr. Robinson, Cole told me to come and help you gather your things."

With shivering lips I began to reply. "Ok, thank you Ashton." I started to grab my things, which consisted of seven large plastic bags and two suitcases. We both grabbed as many as we could, Ashton had already started to go down stairs, and I looked back into my room and turned out my bedroom light. This house was no longer the place where I lived; it's a place where I will leave my soul behind.

I made it down stairs; the front door was open with flashing lights coming from cameras. Ashton came to me; he helped me out of the house, I didn't look back at my parents. I knew my mum was standing at the living room doorway, but I couldn't look at her, I didn't want to look at the women who didn't love me anymore. No parent would dismiss their child from their lives; parents couldn't do that. To me now, I have no family.

A car journey and a flight later, Cole and I made it to France. I am uncertain where we are due to the fact that I slept the entire way. We didn't talk during the journey here, I think Cole understood my silence, because he didn't say a word to me, he let me drift off into a place where I wanted to be, my dreams. Having Cole around me my dreams had gotten better in the previous dreams, because now I know Cole is the one that saved me, I know he would again, so taking that into consideration, I had amazing dreams now. When we got back to the glass villa, Cole directed me in the direction of the bedroom, when we got in there I went and laid down on the four poster bed, Cole came and lay next to me I placed my head on his muscular chest. "I love you." I said proudly.

"I love you more." He kissed my forehead and started to run his fingers through my hair, "how are you feeling?"

"I'm not entirely sure to be honest. I know I made the right choice though, because I couldn't live a lie, I've been doing it too long, I need you Cole more than anything."

"Alec, you have me, and I'm not going anywhere, I promise." Cole announced.

CHAPTER TWENTY-ONE

Five years later....

"Hey Alec are we going to the beach or what I'm not waiting any longer." Elliot's voice came from down stairs. Elliot has become as famous as Cole in the last four years, his voice is now playing across the entire world, with three number one singles and two number one albums, I have never been so happy for him.

"Yeah man I'm on my way, go on a head without me."

"Well hurry up Regan is getting pretty annoyed that she has to wait."

Cole stood in the en-suit of our bedroom in the four-story mansion where we live. He stared at me with loving eyes. "You know just because you're a world renowned author doesn't mean you have to be locked away in this room, we have a family now." He was dressed in jersey shorts and a vest top, looking as handsome as ever.

"Yeah I know I'm just getting back to the author house now, they sent me the latest figures of Dreams. They said it's picked up so much that they want to send it over to china now." My book was released two years ago and now I'm still trying to figure out how my life has changed considerably, I'm nearly as famous as my husband, which is pretty big in the aspects of fame. My book went viral within the first eight months of release, I went on TV shows all around the world, but now it still hasn't settled in. My life has been full of up and downs, but that's ok because life is like that. I have a beautiful family and a perfect best friend. Elliot comes over every summer to our long beach California mansion. Cole and I had made a plan that our summers would be about family when we adopted our daughter Regan, she is the most precious thing in our lives, even Elliot's. When she turned two she said her first word, which was dada, Elliot heard say dada and for a year he was trying to persuade her to say his name, it eventually worked. It has been a ball of laughs to say the least. My mum and dad are no longer in contact with me, I haven't seen or spoken to them in five years, that's the way I want it. My agent told me that my mum has been trying to contact me but I really don't want to hear it. I have my family now; Regan and Cole are the most important people in my life. They make my life complete, and that's all I can ever ask for. Cole's unconditional love for me and Regan has become worldwide news, in May he won the best father award. We both were ecstatic with happiness that we both still laugh about it now four months later. I guess my mum and dad would know about Regan, I wouldn't even think of taking her to see those fools, they had their chance and now I'm laughing at them, and the monsters.

"Ok well I'm ready now, so shall we meet you down there?" Cole asked as walked over to me.

"Yeah you can do, I not be long, Regan's dinner will be ready soon, I'll bring down with me, ok?" I said smiling at him.

"Ok gorgeous, I'll meet you outside. Make sure you don't come down in your boxers I don't want anybody staring at my man." Cole declared proudly, whilst grinning at me.

"Oh shit I forgot, I need to put my shorts on."

Cole Leaned down and kissed me on the forehead whilst looking at the screen of my laptop. "Ok just hurry up please; you know how Regan gets when you're not around."

"Yeah, Yeah I know, I not be long, I promise." I kissed him on lips whilst his teeth were smiling at me, he laughed. "I love you do you know that?"

"I do know that, you tell me every day. I love you too hot stuff." He winked at me and started to leave our room; I turned my head back to my laptop, and began hitting the keys. Cole has become the person I thought Alexis was going to be, he knows the way I work, he knows when I'm hiding my emotions, he knows when I'm stressed out, he knows me. I love that man more than my own life, and to have Regan in our lives is just the icing on the cake, the way he is with her, the way he looks at her, it's like he's found his place in life. His latest album was about our family, and he told it the way a love story should be told. Cole's entire life revolved around fame, but now he has a family, a family that loves him unconditionally. I first met his family when he brought me over here, they are a lovely family, but they don't revolve around family love they revolve around Cole's fame and how much money he makes. I tend to not go around there much, they and I do get along but that is only because they know Cole would dismiss them from his life, which would mean; no money for them. Rocky has been living with us for the entire five years as it is Cole's dog, he guards Regan to the point of chasing away the press, he has a brilliant personality, I have never had a dog before, but he and I have bonded really well.

I finished off my Email, and found my shorts. I walked down the stairs and out into the back yard, which was the beach. Regan and Elliot were playing in the water, Cole was watching from afar, as he watched our daughter play. Elliot saw me and waved, he then knelt down to whisper in Regan's ear, her face lit up as she saw me walking onto the beach. "DADA!" Regan shouted, long blond curls, and tiny frame came running towards me, her laughter was all I could hear.

I started to run towards her, my feet were going as fast as they could, I then falsely fell over, Regan came running and jumped on me, I laughed out loud as she pretended to do CPR, what Cole tort her how to do. At the age of four she has the brains for a thirteen year old, the good thing about her is she didn't go through terrible two's. I was incredibly thankful; I had heard they are like having hell in your home. She became ours three years ago, just after Cole and I got married, ever since she has been the light in our life. "I'm alive, I'm alive." I said breathing heavy. "Oh thank you princess you saved me." I looked up into her deep blue eyes, they always draw me in.

"It's ok dada, I would do it again." Her cute small teeth and cheeks lifted into a smile. She bent down so she could speak into my ear; I slung my arms around her tiny frame. "Dada I know you were prét-ending, I'm not dumb you know." she said making me laugh.

"And how would you know that?"

"Because I do." She got up and started to run back over to Uncle Elliot. I got up as well and started to walk over to Cole.

When I got to him he was smiling at me with his ray bans on and his hair going wild with the wind, he placed his arms up against the wooden part of the shelter shack. "That girl I swear is the smartest child in the world." I laughed.

"I know, tell me about it." He smiled back me, showing his veneer white teeth.

We stayed looking out into the ocean and looking at our baby and Elliot. Life really can throw unexplainable circumstances at you, but at this point in my life, I don't think I could be happier. My daughter will one day learn that her dada was raped, and when that day comes I will be prepared because I'm not afraid of them anymore, they don't have control over me, not any more. My life story is publicly known to the world, yes when it came out I was absolutely petrified. However, I would not change it because it pushed me to do what I want, which was to announce to the world to get every person like them locked away, to give the survivors hope that they can do what I did. I'm reveling in the fact that I helped so many people tell their story, which is a very large part of why I am so happy. Theirs and my life will never be the same again, but from this point on, we can only become stronger. Now is a fresh new start, a new piece of paper, now is the beginning. I am happy.

ABOUT THE AUTHOR

Liam Tyrrell has never attempted to write a book as he never had a story to write about until a traumatic event occurred. He has suffered through pain and lived through it, dealt with it and is now a person who lives each day as if its his last.

Lightning Source UK Ltd.
Milton Keynes UK
UKOW02f2332270616

277216UK00003B/149/P